daniel mueller

anything
you.
recognize

Outpost19 | San Francisco
outpost19.com

ISBN: 9781944853860

Mueller, Daniel
Anything You Recognize / Daniel Mueller

Available in paperback and ebook editions Fall
2023.

Stories included in this book have appeared (or
will) in the following literary journals: "Cache la
Poudre" in *Booth Journal*; "Nothing Has to Happen" in *Free State Review;* "At Least You'll Have
Company," "Antivenom," "The Way They Do
in Movies," and "After Logic" in *Gargoyle*; "The
Palisades" in *Chicago Quarterly Review*; "Ground
School" in *Pithead Chapel*; "The Embers" in *The
Writing Disorder*; "B-Side" in *Solstice: A Magazine
of Diverse Voices*; "When Words Fail" and "Anything You Recognize" in *Manzano Mountain Review;* "An Incision in the Reeds" in *Alaska Quarterly Review;* and "Always Funny" in *b(OINK)*.

OUTPOST19

ORIGINAL PROVOCATIVE READING
SAN FRANCISCO | @OUTPOST19

Advance praise for

anything you recognize

"Reading Daniel Mueller's stunning new story collection ANYTHING YOU RECOGNIZE is like standing alone under a clear night sky and suddenly seeing a bright red flare arc overhead. As it crackles and sparks, you can't help but marvel, to be completely in awe of it. I dare you to lose yourself in this book, to search anywhere among these pages, for what you'll find is that these stories glow with verve and humor. They burn beautifully, too, with Mueller's signature tenderness and intelligence, often centering on the heartache and questions many of us still carry from the wilderness of childhood. Some writers use their gifts to create the illusion of a world, which is, at times, a difficult enough undertaking, but Mueller has done something even greater: he allows us to discover that what is waiting on the other side of these singular stories is, and has always been, ourselves. I didn't want this book to end, and in the most vital way, it doesn't."
— **Jon Pineda**, author of *Let's No One Get Hurt*

"Dan Mueller's ANYTHING YOU RECOGNIZE is the work of a mature writer at the height of considerable powers, whose subject is America. What made me love this book was its pervading joyfulness. Mueller doesn't shy away from

human suffering—neither the suffering his characters experience nor that they cause. But even in their darkest moments—and there are several—an overtone of cosmic laughter rings in the background. Mueller holds his people to account, but never ceases to extend them the humane and beautiful acceptance these stories offer us."
– **David Payne**, author of *Barefoot to Avalon, Early from the Dance,* and *Ruin Creek*

"These sexy, poignant, unpredictable stories explode quietly across the pages, shards ripping into the vulnerable, often dark, underbelly of the American Dream. I can't stop thinking about these people. I feel like I've met them, grown up with them...and maybe been them."
— **Tom Coash**, international, award-winning playwright of *Veils* and *Cry Havoc*

"…heaps of praise for ANYTHING YOU RECOGNIZE and the startling ways in which its elegantly composed stories—funny and heartbreaking, innocent yet laced with menace—lay bare the yearnings and secrets of middle-class Americans. Dan Mueller may be the steeped-in-darkness nephew of Garrison Keillor."
— **Elizabeth Evans**, author of *As Good As Dead, Carter Clay,* and *Suicide's Girlfriend*

"An artful and unflinching examination of life's oft-obscured lines between convention and morality, human fragility and resilience. These 15 stories comprise a vivid portrait of childhood

joys and dangers, young love, and mature loss, including the navigations of youth, boyhood, race, truth, and the relationships that ultimately define and then break us. With exquisite detail and prose to savor, ANYTHING YOU RECOG-NIZE is a masterclass in the art of short fiction."
— NYT bestselling author **Tosca Lee**, author of *Demon: A Memoir, Havah, Iscariot, The Progeny,* and *The Line Between*

"Never predictable, these stories trumpet the pleasures and troubles of adulthood, often encountered by a curious young boy who is both drawn to and repelled by the mysteries of desire, sexuality, morality, love, and heartbreak. The stunning sentences in Mueller's ANY-THING YOU RECOGNIZE will guide you deftly into stories that end in a gut-punch, leaving you feeling surprised, raw, and awestruck, a greater understanding of the human experience having passed like a ghost before you."
— **Kim Henderson**, author of *The Kind of Girl*

"Dan Mueller's latest collection of stories, his third, will likely propel him into the upper echelon of contemporary short story writers, alongside Richard Ford, Alice Munro, Lorrie More, George Saunders, Jhumpa Lahiri, Junot Diaz, Aimee Bender and others in that elegant constellation. He has what they all have, a style and a voice that belongs to him alone. His char-acters grow out of a vibrant mulch of living details of their lives; and when you think you

know exactly what will push itself through the soil, something unexpected arises. The turns in Mueller's stories do not come with the blare of trumpets, sometimes rather from a subordinate clause that snaps your head back and you say what just happened! He finds poetry in nature, not with inflated prose, but in noticing the unexpected way in which things live. Several, though not all, of the stories are set during one character's childhood in a military camp. Like all the stories in this collection, they contain events we may expect to be there, but only as a launchpad for some gorgeous, unexpected rippling harmonic that tears out an old wall in the heart and replaces it with a shot of life. For readers looking to be moved, transported, riveted; you will find those experiences within these pages. For writers looking for a master class, this is your 8 credit course."
— **Hal Ackerman**, author of *The Art of the First Draft*

"Dan Mueller's stories in ANYTHING YOU RECOGNIZE delight in precision, in words and their sounds, like "narthex" and "crankbait." I shook my head with laughter at so many startling sentences which build the worlds of characters full of longing for home and companionship and left me moved and contemplative, wondering at life and its beauty and strangeness."
— **Greg Martin**, author of *Stories for Boys* and *Mountain City*

anything
you
recognize

And each separate dying ember wrought its
ghost upon the floor.

Edgar Allan Poe

Contents

Cache la Poudre

I

Built into every home was an incinerator. Ours was outside in the back of the house, flush with the bricks, a toaster-sized cast iron compartment into which I stuffed The Greeley Tribune, old issues of Look and Time, grocery bags, cardboard, and mail, and set it all ablaze with a kitchen match. While I was expected to load the dishwasher after supper, make my bed every morning, and pick up after myself when I played, incinerating the paper trash was the one chore that never seemed onerous.

Throughout the week tender collected in the breezeway, and on Saturday mornings as my parents slept, after Jonny Quest and Aquaman, I carried it onto the back porch and stacked it on the cement under the cast iron door on which was molded in raised lettering:

AMERICAN INCINERATOR CORP.
DETROIT   NEW YORK

The inside was thick with soot, and as I filled it with wadded pages, struck the tip of a match against the strip of flint and transferred the flame to a corner of crumpled newsprint, I was careful not to touch the top or sides. A dab of blackness on a fingertip could mean later being told I'd ruined a couch or chair as my mother scrubbed the upholstery with a sponge.

Once started, the fire consumed all that I fed it, at the darting pinnacle of each blue-orange petal a tendril of smoke that coiled with the others into a rope God pulled hand over hand up the flue. These were the souls He'd spared from eternal torment, in the oven, misshapen and buckling, the ones He hadn't, and as bits of ash floated around me, I thought of them as angels come to spectate, the drama unfolding in my recessed stage so captivating not even God's minions could look away.

When I was through, my father paid me my weekly allowance, usually two quarters but sometimes an Eisenhower fifty-cent piece that I squeezed between my eyebrow and cheek and wore like a monocle, thinking myself a comedian.

On Saturdays, I walked with my next-door-neighbor David Ratcliff the three blocks to Rexall Drug where in the toy aisle were novelties we coveted, most priced beyond our means. Oak-handled bullwhips. Model funny cars. Trick playing cards. Silly Putty. But once, rather than blowing our money on comic books and candy like we usually did, we saved our earnings and pooled them together, and at the end of two pay periods we bought a slingshot.

The frame cut in China from substandard plywood, sturdy rubber bands stapled to the prongs, it wasn't the highest quality slingshot, but as David and I took turns firing stones at targets near and far in the vacant lots across the street from our houses, we were impressed by its range if not its accuracy. We missed everything at which we aimed except the ground and sky, and we shot at the latter just to marvel at how high and long a stone would soar. Our terrible marksmanship notwithstanding, we understood we possessed a lethal weapon and, by extension, the power to kill, and were careful not to point the slingshot at each other or fire a stone straight up.

His mother rang the dinner bell, and we flipped a coin to see which of us would keep the slingshot overnight. "Heads I win, tails you lose," David said, a joke that always made us laugh. As the nickel flipped through the air, I called tails and won.

That night I slept with the slingshot under my pillow, a cat's eye marble clutched in my fist, imagining my left arm straight and level with my shoulder, my ammo pulled back to my ear, and between the uprights the guilty face of the burglar I was certain would come for my mother's jewelry, my father's fly rod, our television set and stereo now that I had the means to apprehend him and bring him to justice. The next morning, I dressed in my church clothes and checked to see whether anything had been taken from our sleeping house. Nothing had, and I crept outside through the front door.

On our front stoop, I trained the slingshot at the 14th Street and 17th Avenue street signs that formed a cross marking our corner lot, pulled back the bands, and watched my cat's eye marble deflect off a fire hydrant, arc over a teal Chevelle parked crookedly in a neighbor's driveway, and land in the vacant lots in a wisp of dust. I recovered it in the dirt before the opening to one of many tunnels that led to underground caverns my parents forbade me from entering, afraid earth would collapse around me and bury me alive. Though I burrowed into them regularly without their knowledge, if I did so in my church clothes there'd be hell to pay. So, I shot at bags caught in bushes, hearts carved into the trunks of trees, an old refrigerator lying on its back, the door removed so no kids would climb into it and make it their coffin. When no shot hit its mark, I tried to compensate for the weapon's inaccuracy by firing above and below my targets, to the left and right of them, but there was no accounting for its poor performance. If I fired left, the projectile went right or even farther left. If I fired up, it went down or even father up.

My marble lost after the second shot, steam no doubt rising from the silver dollar pancakes my mother prepared for our breakfast before church on Sundays, I started back to the house and was nearly home when on a lower branch of the big oak I could see from our picture window a robin sang, its breast puffed. I picked up a stone, placed it in the pouch, pulled back the bands as I'd imagined doing the night before in an act of heroism. When the bird filled the V that rose from my clenched fist, I relaxed my thumb and forefinger and launched the stone into its head. In a flutter of wings, it dropped from the tree, and I stood over it disbelieving as blood leaked from its beak into the dirt.

From then on, I no longer thought of myself as one of the souls God saved from the flames but one of those He left to burn.

II

The first time it happened was in the parking lot of Cattleman's Steakhouse on the outskirts of town. We'd gone there to celebrate my fifth birthday, and after supper on the way back to our car, a peppermint candy I'd pilfered from the bowl beside the cash register slithered off the root of my tongue and caught in my throat. I don't remember gagging or otherwise expressing alarm. Before I could do either, I was hung upside down by my ankles, the covered wagon outside the restaurant jerking up and down as the lozenge dropped from my pharynx onto the roof of my mouth. I flicked it with my tongue and heard it clack on the asphalt.

My father, a doctor, set me down beside the red- and white-striped pinwheel. The size of a nickel and speckled with dirt, it glistened with saliva like something coughed up by the sea.

My mother knelt beside me and put her palm to my forehead. "He started to gag," my father explained. "What did you expect me to do, Linda?"

"Are you all right?" she asked me.

"I'm fine," I said, stood up and brushed myself off. "See? Good as new."

She wrapped her arms around my father

and kissed his cheek, and I was pleased to have given him the opportunity to perform an act of valor, but in the car on our way home, he said, "It's a good thing the candy came out. If it hadn't, I would've had to perform an emergency tracheotomy right there in the parking lot."

These were the days of hard candies lodging in my windpipe regularly. My favorite was butterscotch, but not one to turn down sugar in any form I choked on grape, cinnamon, strawberry, cherry. Candy jars, made of china or tinted glass, could be found in most living rooms, usually on an end table or coffee table, and when you lifted the lid as you might a bough from a robin's nest, the hard candies in their metallic wrappers— honey yellow, imperial blue, royal purple—glimmered in the daylight that filtered through drapes and blinds onto drab friezes and abrasive boucles.

"What's a tracheotomy?" I asked.

In the rearview mirror I met my father's eyes, the lenses of his glasses reflecting the numbers of the lit speedometer. In the twilight, the northern Colorado sky was smeared with paint and even the cattle in their feedlots were infused with indigo, pink, red.

"Put your fingers to your throat and find the soft spot where your neck joins your chest. It'll be just above where your clavicles come together."

"Jim," my mother cautioned.

"It's OK, Linda," he said. "Did you find it?" I nodded.

"That's your trachea, also known as your windpipe. If the candy hadn't dislodged, I would've had to force the casing of a ballpoint pen into your neck at that very spot."

"Why?" I asked.

"Because otherwise you'd suffocate. The candy was obstructing the flow of air to your lungs, and if it hadn't dislodged, I would've had to create an alternate duct."

At home the next day I unscrewed the upper and lower halves of a ballpoint pen and, peering through the cylinder that tapered to a hole, imagined seeing the hidden world that lay beneath the skin, the trachea that led downward to the lungs, expanding and contracting within a cage of ribs that expanded and contracted to accommodate them, and upward to the larynx, out of which my voice came whenever I spoke, sang, hummed, yelled, cried, or laughed. While I didn't want one in my trachea, I liked looking through it. Whatever appeared in the opening—the dial of the television set on which my parents and I watched The Ed Sullivan Show, our TV dinners before us on TV trays, or the new robin in the oak that shaded the vacant lots where tunnels, dug into the hard clay by kids who'd come before us, led to caverns into which a kid could snake and vanish from sight—seemed more mysterious when isolated from the things around it.

If ABC, CBS, and NBC each had its own channel, what were the other numbers on the dial for? And if a robin choked on a seed, did it know what to do to save itself?

III

The Ratcliffs were Mormons, and the day before David Ratcliff's older brother Ken left on a two-year mission to Stockholm, Sweden, his parents threw a backyard potluck. While Mr. Ratcliff barbecued chicken on a grill, four card tables draped with red-checkered tablecloths became bamboo cages into which David and I retreated with our plates heaped high. Above us lay the buffet, and as neighbors helped themselves to three types of potato salad, three types of bean salad, three types of Jell-O salad, and a platter of charred breasts, thighs, wings, and drumsticks, we pretended they were our captors and we POW's like the ones in the Fightin' Army comic books we hid beneath our mattresses lest our mothers discover reading material they thought "picayune" and "beneath" us. More than once they'd marched us each to the incinerator and made us look on as pages of splendid gore erupted into flames turned jungle green, river blue, desert brown by the ink.

In the gap between tablecloth and grass, the enemy had slipped us rations meant to keep us alive and susceptible to the tortures they had in store for us: taped to our fingers firecrackers lit one by one until we "talked," fishhooks lancing our genitals tugged until we confessed our unit's coordinates, chopsticks inserted ever deeper into our rectums until we divulged state secrets, our imaginations limitless when devising our own agonies. Not David's teenaged sister Janice in her Monkees flip-flops, not my mother's coral Mary

Janes nor my father's suede leather cowboy boots could dissuade us from the delusion of our captivity.

"If we can just hold on until nightfall, we'll be free," David said and sank his teeth into an ear of corn. "Look, I've cut through my shackles."

"So have I," I said and raised my wrists and ankles.

"Once everyone's asleep, we'll SNAP these prison bars LIKE TWIGS!"

Only plump Mrs. Cosgrove and her wide feet squeezed into mauve slippers embroidered with mustard blossoms interrupted our drama. It wasn't that we didn't like her. We did, especially the butterscotch hard candies she kept in a milk glass urn and offered to us whenever she invited us to sit with her in her living room. It was her grandson Jerry who mortified us, and if she was ladling creamed spinach onto a paper plate from the enamel porringer above us, he wasn't far away. We glanced over our shoulders, and our suspicions were confirmed by his black Keds on the grass behind us, the eyelets free of lacing and tongues akimbo.

"Where are they?" he asked his grandmother.

"Oh, I'm pretty sure they're here somewhere," she replied. To Mrs. Cosgrove Jerry had been entrusted by the State of Colorado for reasons he refused to disclose, though he loved telling us how much better life was "up north" in Cheyenne where his dad worked in the oilfields or "out east" in Brush where his mom waitressed at a truck stop. Only a year older than David and me, Jerry was a third taller than either of us, with sinewy arms and legs that could outperform our undeveloped ones whether we were playing ball or wrestling on the lawn. No matter the contest, he always won, and while our pride suffered, the injuries to it were nothing compared to the smarting palms left by his fastballs, the stinging nipples left by his spirals, the grass-stained abrasions left by his guillotine chokes and Indian deathlocks.

"We're not getting out of here anytime soon," David whispered, invisible bindings marrying his wrists and ankles anew. It was summer solstice, the longest day of the year, and unless we wanted Jerry to remind us of the difference between our scrawny bodies and the rippling ones of PFC Tony Ardino and Lieutenant John Clay, whose muscles bulged from their tattered battledress, we might have to remain in hiding for hours.

I lay on my side. "Guess I'll get some shut-eye," I said and farted.

"Uh-oh," David said. "Nerve gas."

On the grass not twenty feet away, my three-year-old sister Elaine sat with her back to us. Before her sat Jerry, kneecaps glistening on either side of her, her head a blond ball of twine on which his catlike eyes were fixed. He gnawed on a drumstick, a smile drawing to his cheeks his tear-shaped dimples. "Hand me the binocs, Ardino!" I said and David passed me the pop-up opera glasses with which his mother identified migrating birds. The collapsible binoculars were the size of a cigarette case, but when a button was pressed on the top of them, lenses sprang up between the panels, and what you held was a lopsided sand-wich of vinyl, chrome, and glass. Should Jerry turn on my sister, as he did on us, I would come to her rescue.

I put the glasses to my eyes, and Jerry's wide brow, across which brown bangs hung like matchsticks, his mirthful grin and broad, laugh-ing shoulders filled my vision. Though I couldn't see my sister's face, from her fluttering elbows I could tell that she was feeding it, and no more afraid of Jerry than she was of me.

That's when I saw the tick, a beige, crescent-shaped garlic clove attached to her right earlobe. Jerry saw it, too, and once his expression had changed from bemusement to curiosity to alarm, he screamed my father's name. "Come quick! A giant tick's got Elaine!"

Adults gathered around them, reminding each other of the Rocky Mountain Spotted Fever epidemic we were in. Curling over her like the caring older brother I wasn't, Jerry gently dis-played on the pads of his fingertips my sister's earlobe and the engorged parasite affixed to it.

"Nice work, Jerry," my father said as he picked Elaine up in his arms. He would drive her to the clinic where he worked and extract the tick himself, careful to remove the head from which a whole new body could sprout.

IV

If left in our house unattended, I might spend the

time there on my mother's side of my parents' closet, and between dresses that retained just a soupçon of the verbena she spritzed onto her wrists and neck swathe myself in fabrics I didn't dare to remove from their hangers. Or sit before her vanity table where, having pulled out a pearl-handled drawer, delight in necklaces bestrewn across black velvet. Or uncap a lipstick, turn the bottom, and wonder at a blossoming tulip.

No one had told me that what I was doing was wrong. I felt the horror of it in the pit of my stomach as I crept down the hallway to the master bedroom where the treasures were stored, listening for the grumbling of our Volkswagen squareback shutting off on the driveway and the slamming of car doors, my mother's return from Piggly Wiggly or J. C. Penny. She'd holler at me to help her with her bags, and out I'd run, a smiling Johnny glad to be of service.

One day a dress of turquoise sequins slipped onto the floor, and too short to reach the hanger rod, I laid the garment on the bed, frustrated by my height and furious at my own carelessness. If I could not return the dress to its rightful place, how would I explain to my mother that it had fallen, for what had I been doing in my parents' closet at all? Still, as I admired how sunlight through the blinds fell in bars across the sequins and the lit ones twinkled back as rose and daffodil, calm rationality overtook me. If my secret vice would be discovered anyway, why not, this once and never again, indulge it?

Soon my shorts, underpants, and t-shirt lay

in a little pile at my feet as the hem of the dress yawned above me. I let it drop, and as it enveloped me, I felt as if I were diving upward into a swimming pool, even the charmeuse lining water-like and refreshing. A sundress on my mother, falling to her upper thigh, on me was a formal gown. At her vanity table, I applied powder to my face, blush to my cheeks, black eyeliner above and below my lashes and white at the inner corners of my eyes, eye shadow, electric blue wings to match my irises, and to my lips a pale pink hue that I outlined in red pencil the way I'd watched my mother do her own. I slipped onto a wrist a silver charm bracelet from which dangled a wishing well, shamrock, heart, thimble, fish, and horseshoe. Around my neck I draped five strands of faux pearls and to my earlobes clipped gold plated faux pearl daisies. Unrecognizable to myself in the chalkware mirror, I blew myself a kiss.

In the afternoon when my father returned with his partner Dr. Cook from fly-fishing the South Platte River between Cache la Poudre and Big Thompson Creek where Dr. Cook owned sixty acres of pasture, I was dancing in the living room to The King and I soundtrack and singing "Getting to Know You" with Deborah Kerr. Waders slung over his shoulder and wicker creel bounding from his hip, my father minced up the walk toward the front stoop. I saw him through the storm door, but so immersed was I in the menagerie of exotically costumed children I'd traveled to Siam to teach that I'd forgotten I was even wearing my mother's clothes, make up, and jewelry or the trepidation with which I'd first put them on.

"Because of all," I sang, "the beautiful and new, things I'm learning about you... da-a-ay by da-a-ay!"

My father entered the living room, his expression a knot of incomprehension, revulsion, and fear. But he balanced his fly rod on top of the television set, unloaded his waders and creel, and went back outside. "Don, something's come up," I heard him say.

"I hope nothing's wrong, Jim."

Through the storm door I watched him put his arm around Dr. Cook's shoulders as he walked him back to the station wagon parked curbside. I turned off the record player and stood over seven brook trout that, in my father's haste, had spilled from the creel onto the carpet. Leaves and grass stuck to their speckled blue sides and blood orange bellies, and the slender fillet knife with which he'd cleaned them lay sheathed among their tails and fins. Though my mother would not like finding fish on Saxony she vacuumed twice a week, I was afraid to touch them.

When my father came back inside, he squatted before the creel, and as he returned the trout to it, he said, "You aren't a girl. You can't—I can't have you dressing like that." When he looked up, we were eye to eye, and his cheeks were pinstriped. Though I was still the same old Travis he'd known since my birth, it felt as if I were looking at him through the wrong end of a telescope and he was far, far away, even as I smelled the fish on his hands and from the stain they'd left on the carpet.

"Do you understand me?" he said.

I nodded.

"It's a lot to take in for someone your age, I know. But I need you to be a man. I need you to be the man. Your mother has your little sister to look after. You're going to have to help her, as I would if I were here."

"But you are here," I replied.

"I won't be for long. In six weeks, I report for Basic Training. We're moving to Fort Hood, Texas. Your mother knows. We've been waiting for the right time to tell you."

"But I like Greeley," I said.

"I like Greeley, too," he said. "Now let's get you cleaned up before your mother and sister return."

At my father's command, I raised my arms, and with a whoosh! I was nude, the sundress in his hand as natural there as the chamois with which he wiped beads of hose water from our car's finish. He ran a bath for me, scrubbed my face hard with a washcloth, and by the time my mother and sister returned, all evidence of my crime had been expunged.

Even the carpet stain was gone.

V

I didn't know how to tell David Ratcliff that my family was moving out-of-state, and in the end, I didn't have to. My mother spoke to his mother, and his mother spoke to him, and the day the

15

Mayflower men parked their van in front of our house, David and I crept through tunnels in the clay to our favorite cavern.

"Don't you just wish the earth would cave in around us and bury us alive?" he asked.

To us the vacant lots were a dinosaur burial ground. Our backs rested against walls worn smooth by our visits, and dust hung suspended in two pillars of sunlight that fell from the eye sockets of a stegosaurus, holes that sometimes snagged our feet when we walked above ground. Below it, we were paleontologists surrounded by skeletons that lent architecture to the passageways through which we crawled and the rooms in which we hunkered.

"We're friends for life, right?" I said. "No matter where we are or where we go, we are each other's first friend, best friend, last friend. First, best, last, right?" I tried to get him to shake on it as we'd done many times before, but he only drew his knees to his forehead and shut his eyes. "Ok, what do you say we measure our dicks?" I said to cheer him up. For a while, pulling our penises to see how far they'd stretch had been his favorite pastime, but today he only cocked his head and said,

"We didn't bring a ruler."

"Rulery foolery," I said. "We can measure them against each other." I scooted out from my shorts and underwear, felt the coolness of the earth against my buttocks and the air against my privates. "Come on," I said, "there's mine. Show me yours."

He glanced at it with mild amusement. "What's the point? Later today you'll be gone, and everything we did together will seem like a dream, a dream that was too good to be true, and in time even it will be forgotten."

"Nothing will be forgotten," I said. "And when we're grown, we'll buy side-by-side mansions, just like we planned."

"Remember," he said, "when I saved your life? When you choked on a lemon drop and I slapped your back until it popped onto the lawn?"

"I'll never forget that."

"Or when Mrs. Cosgrove sent Jerry after us for scaring her half to death with window rattlers?"

"And we hid from him in this very cavern?"

"And the moon filled it with silvery light?"

"I won't forget that either."

"You might not right away. But in six weeks? Two years? Ten years?"

A turkey vulture, its head a drop of blood pricked from the sky, coursed from one of the stegosaurus's eye sockets to the other.

"Think of how many times we shook hands on promises. Too many times to count. Which means they've all merged into a single handshake and the actual ones that meant so much to us at the time have already been forgotten. If we can't even remember those, how will we remember anything once we're separated by all the miles and time?"

"Pull your pants down," I told him. When he refused, I said, "If you want our promise to each other to be unforgettable, you'll pull them down."

He crinkled his nose, across which a dozen freckles were scattered, as he reluctantly complied.

"Now grab your dick and repeat after me, 'First, best, last.'" As he did, I rolled on top of him and touched my penis to his. "First, best, last," I said, and he did, too. "First! Best! Last!" I chanted, and he chanted, too, and when I rolled off him, we were half in shadow, and Jerry's grinning face filled the aperture above us.

"Gentlemen," he said, his breath smelling of breakfast sausage, bits of which were caught between his teeth. "Three can play this game." David jerked to sitting and yanked his pants to his waist, but I took my time with mine. I was moving to Texas, my father was already there, and while Jerry could hold what he'd seen over David, he couldn't over me.

"Leave us alone," David said. "Nobody invited you."

"Nobody had to invite me," Jerry replied. "The tunnels belong to everyone." When blue sky again filled the hole, we knew he was coming after us.

Two passageways led to the cavern. Jerry would take the shorter. "Come on," I whispered and started crawling through the longer toward light that filtered through the opening that led to the ground.

"He's got my foot," David said behind me, "Jerry's got my foot," but I kept crawling and when I rose from the hole, I was by myself, and my mother was calling to me.

"It's time to go!"

"Bye," I said to my friend.

The Embers

At potlucks you never failed to evoke the flesh
and blood of the living Christ.

Once all were seated at card tables in the
church basement before plates heaped with Ann
Constable's meatloaf, Ruth Goetzman's chicken
casserole, Helen Wolfe's deviled ham puffs, Mar-
go Humphrey's German stew, and my then-wife
Lorna's short ribs, seared in batches on the stove
and braised in the oven in tomato sauce seasoned
with Tabasco, with arms outstretched and palms
to the ceiling you asked the Lord to bless our
food and reminded us that it was, in sacramen-
tal terms, no different from the morsels of bread
and thimbles of grape juice distributed during
communion. A skeptic at best, I said my "Amen"
with the others and tried to ignore any pangs of
conscience, but never forgetting that in Dante's
Inferno the lowest circle of Hell is reserved for
hypocrites.

Dinners at your home, on the other hand,
were served without a word of grace. You and Bev
were close in age to Lorna and me, your daughters
Holly and Jill close in age to our sons Luke and
Vance, and in addition to the canoe trips down the
Saint Croix River our families took together each
autumn to admire the colors, every six weeks you
would join us for supper at our house or we'd
join you at yours. Still, as much as our families
enjoyed each other, I'd come to dread the moment

when, our wives and children having retired to their respective domains, you would say, "May I have a word with you, Bruce?"

"Sure, Myron," I'd say. Then we'd descend the stairs to one or the other of our partially modeled basements, to one or the other of our paneled offices, mine displaying in a locked mahogany gun rack the Browning 30-30 deer rifle and Remington 12 gauge pheasant gun that had followed me from childhood, though I'd lost all interest in hunting after the boys were born, yours displaying a framed diploma from Wesley Theological Seminary in Washington D. C. and many of the same photographs that decorated the walls of the church's narthex, of you robed and beaming beside tiers of confirmands, teenagers in dresses or suits and ties with hair that seemed to grow in length and breadth with each successive class. In the lower right corner of each was a placard listing the name of our church, Good Sam United Methodist, and the year of the confirmation.

Three pastors had preceded you since the church's inception in 1953, but since 1968, the year I was released from the service, moved my family to Minnesota, and first went into private practice, you'd been our flock's shepherd, and I knew no one to speak ill of you.

By turns self-deprecating and welcoming, in thick-lensed glasses that magnified your eyes to twice their natural size, you had the air of a counselor to whom much had been entrusted. I was grateful, as I'm sure you were, that most of our conversations were light. As we waited for Lorna

and Bev to call us to dinner, we discussed whether the Vikings, your team, had a better chance of
making the playoffs than the Packers, mine, some
state and national politics but in strokes broad
enough to leave the question of whether we agreed
on fundamentals to the imagination, musky fishing, and church business, whether I thought replacing the carpeting in the aisles and nave a wor-
thy investment of church capital, which I did not,
or whether more money should be channeled into
church youth programs, which I did. The only
OB-GYN who was also a regular church member, I was the one you called upon to talk to each
confirmation class about sex, not the mechanics
of it, which by fifteen and sixteen all should have
known, but the joy of it when shared with the
right partner at the right time and, of course, the
risks. Years before the outbreak of AIDS, I recited
the litany of garden variety venereal diseases of
which they needed to be aware and outlined the
standard methods of birth control, from I.U.D.s
to the pill and from condoms, diaphragms, and
spermicidal jelly to sterilization by vasectomy or
tubal ligation, and—while not the most exciting
method known to humankind, I told them, certainly the most effective—abstinence.

If the termination of a pregnancy, also
known as an abortion, was in the strict sense a
method of birth control, I told them that I'd performed them only under the direst circumstances,
when the mother's life had been endangered by
an ectopic pregnancy, for instance, or when diag-
nostic tests had detected in the fetus a fatal genetic

disorder like trisomy 18 or a fatal disease like Tay Sachs, and would not perform them just because the mother, regardless of her age or station, didn't wish to see her pregnancy through to term. This was a lie, of course. And you, who during each of my talks had sat with the kids in the living room of Yahweh House, a forest green bungalow bequeathed to the church by Delores Peacock upon her death at age 92, knew it. You knew it not because I'd confessed to you the guilt I'd felt at performing them, though I had. You knew it because both—there had been two—I'd performed at your request on the teenaged daughters of prominent church members.

In both cases, the parents of the pregnant girl had come to you for counseling, and while I wasn't privy to your conversations, I'm sure you recited their options, including keeping the baby—it would be their grandchild after all—or putting it up for adoption.

From our conversations, I gleaned that neither girl's parents had been in favor of her seeing the pregnancy through to term. When I met with the girls themselves to discuss the procedure, neither, in truth, were they. Everyone involved, parents and patients both, agreed that to spare the girls the stigma and shame associated with their conditions their pregnancies should be terminated at the earliest opportunity, and not at an abortion clinic with Right-to-Lifers lying in wait to harangue and harass them but at a doctor's office in an upscale OB-GYN clinic befitting their upbringing and class. And because of my reputation as a doctor and church member, you felt that I should be the one to do it.

The problem was, except in the instances cited in each of my sex talks, I had not performed an abortion on any of my own patients who had elected to have one but had referred them instead to the one partner of the eight of us at the clinic, Dr. Heath, who performed D and C's discretely when he felt the situation required it and took, I think, some pride in the work, believing the Supreme Court ruling in Roe versus Wade toothless without physicians willing to handle the demand. In truth, Myron, my aversion to terminating a healthy pregnancy had nothing to do with the Supreme Court ruling—I believed then as now in a woman's sovereignty over her own body—but rather in the part of the Declaration of Geneva that reads, "I will maintain the utmost respect for human life."

All of this I explained to you, the first time in your office, the second time in mine, in the half-light from our desk lamps while we waited for our wives to call us to dinner, and both times you absorbed every word, your closely cropped head bowed toward your lap, your khaki trousers crossed at your knees, the grooves from your cheekbones to your chin carved, one never doubted, by the deep well of your sympathy and your desire to help those of your flock in need.

"Could you think of this, Bruce," you said both times after I had finished, "as a form of tithing? Because that's what it is. A tithe, an offering, a very generous gift."

And both times that was how I viewed what I then agreed to do.

•

Between the first two abortions you asked me to perform and the third, six years elapsed. The church grew—our kids grew, too—and while I hadn't washed the taste of the first two abortions from my mouth, I assumed you'd taken what I'd told you to heart and realized that despite my calling I wasn't cut out for tithes of this magnitude. Another OB-GYN, Sunny Li, and her husband Niles, a radiologist, had moved to Minneapolis from Illinois and joined Good Sam in the meantime, and it occurred to me that perhaps you'd turned to her for assistance. Confirmation classes had more than doubled in size, such that the synod had assigned the church a youth minister to assist with the religious instruction, and the cultural endorsement of sex without consequence, ubiquitous in cinema, television, pop music, and advertising, hadn't made being a teenager any easier.

Indeed, when Lorna handed me a copy of Hustler Magazine our younger son had squirreled away on the top shelf of his closet beneath a stack of Sports Illustrateds, I was as shocked as she by the explicit nature of the "artwork" inside—vaginas splayed open by airbrushed fingernails, cameras positioned no further away from their subjects than I was from mine during pelvic exams, even the urethra, a speck, discernible to the least trained eye. Though I joked, "I had no idea Vance was remotely interested in his old man's line of work," and suggested returning the contraband to its hiding place, reluctant as I was to eradicate an outlet that, rechanneled, might lead to graver outcomes, I was saddened by the absence of subtlety, even if by today's standards the photos might seem as antiquated and quaint as the pornographic cabinet cards my own father kept behind the bar as curiosities he pulled out for the amusement of patrons in the 40's and 50's.

Behind my parents' tavern in Wausau, Wisconsin had stood the icehouse, and one of my jobs as a kid had been to chop ice for the wells from blocks nestled in the straw.

While filling the wells from buckets one day, I told Lorna as I passed Vance's magazine back to her, I first encountered the set of silver gelatin prints of female nudes—"naked ladies," my friends and I called them—perched on divans as they smoked cigarettes at the ends of long holders or inserted hairpins into tresses before Baroque vanities. None of the women were entirely nude—each was draped in a bed sheet or strings of pearls—and yet once seen I couldn't erase them from my mind, the shadowed loins, the thinly sheathed breasts and nipples, the powdered expressions of knowing nonchalance.

"So that's why you became an OB-GYN," Lorna said. "It all suddenly makes perfect sense."

It was a Saturday afternoon in the summer of 1980. The lawns were mown, front, back, and sides, the edges trimmed, and the boys had taken the Volvo, Luke in the driver's seat, to Bush Lake to wash the grass stains from their ankles and forearms. I laughed, and Lorna did, too. Then she said, "Oh my God, Bruce, will you look at these?" and displayed a section of the magazine called "Beaver Hunt," which featured snapshots that women from across the United States and Canada had had taken of themselves and mailed to the publisher, each with her legs parted as if by invisible stirrups, for the $150 that would be hers if her photo was run.

Some sat on ratty sofas or chairs. Others rested on filthy shag. One I remember to this day lay sprawled across a child's inflatable bathing pool, her tropical-colored bikini wadded on the grass beside her feet. At first, I thought she was Katie Schnegel, an OR nurse with whom I was having an affair and, in truth, had slept that morning after rounds. Poor as the photo's quality was, the crazy, gap-toothed, take-no-prisoners smile was pure Katie. So, too, the brown pigtails. And yet upon closer inspection, a jack-o-lantern's grin of keloids at the base of the subject's mound of Venus, presumably from a poorly incised Cesarean, differentiated her from Katie, who was childless. Lorna, ever curious, wanted to know at which of the photos I was looking, and I tapped it with my finger. By then she was sitting in the chair beside mine at our kitchen table, squinting at the citations beneath the photos.

"Don't tell me you recognize B.K. from Vancouver, British Columbia," she said.

"I thought she was a patient is all," I said.

"But she can't be, not if she lives in Canada, right?"

"You know who she looks like?" Lorna said. "Katie Schnegel, the OR nurse you introduced me to at the hospital."

A month before, when the Mercedes dealership had been out of loaners, Lorna had picked me up after surgery as I was saying goodbye to Katie.

"Honestly, the resemblance would never have occurred to me, honey," I said.

"Are you kidding?" Lorna said, "It looks just like her," and I agreed, not about to point out the telltale scar that followed B.K.'s swimsuit line or, having by then scrutinized the image more closely, the mole on her vulva and larger-than-average clitoral hood.

Instead, I closed the magazine and said, "Escarpment," an innocent enough word that not long before had fallen outside either of our children's vocabularies and, because Lorna and I had both liked the sound of it, was code for: Let's make love at the first available opportunity. When our kids were younger, they, too, had delighted in the word and neither of us had felt the least compunction to give it context, both of us blurting it apropos of nothing. But as Vance and Luke matured, we had to become more sophisticated in our usage, reminiscing about the escarpments we had seen on vacations—the Mogollan Rim in Arizona, for instance, or Devil's Slide in California—or would, we imagined, on vacations to come—the Serra da Mantiqueira in Brazil, Baltic

Klint in Sweden, or Côte d'Or in France.

"Can't you be any more original than that?" Lorna said.

"Under pressure, sure," I said, and we retired to our bedroom, but not before returning Vance's magazine to his bedroom closet.

In contrast to our working-class parents, we saw ourselves as enlightened, and after all the talks about sex we'd had with our sons, their private lives were their business, we agreed, not ours.

•

The third abortion I performed at your request was on Teri, the 15-year-old daughter and only child of Glen and Myrna, who belonged to our church bridge group. All four couples were members, and while before and after services the wives planned each month's bridge party, once we squared off in the four cardinal directions with our decks of playing cards and bowls of chocolate espresso beans, conversation ended, so well matched and competitive were we. Though friendly with Glen and Myrna, I knew little about them other than that he was a tax attorney with a high-powered law firm downtown and she, unlike the other wives, worked, in her case as a French literature professor at a small liberal arts college in Saint Paul. Neither parent accompanied Teri to her consultation, which I thought strange since without a consent form signed by one of them, I could not legally perform the procedure.

When I repeated this to Teri, who sat in my office in a chair across the desk from me as a clinician observed our proceedings from a second chair beside the coat tree, Teri replied, "No worries there. They're Vulcans."

"From Star Trek, the television series?" I asked.

"No," she replied, "from Vulcan, the planet."

"I see," I said.

It was August, and I wondered if she'd attended the sex talk I'd given to the confirmation class in February. I had no recollection of seeing her there or, for that matter, ever seeing her before, not even at Glen and Myrna's the half dozen times our bridge group had convened there. She was a pudgy thing, not from her pregnancy, for she was barely six weeks into her first trimester, but from baby fat that had retained a vestigial hold on her cheeks, arms, and thighs, all flushed from the eleven miles she'd pedaled across town on a girl's five-speed Huffy she'd left in the waiting room propped against a ficus plant. A Ziggy t-shirt enveloped her like a sack, and stenciled onto the violet fabric was the fleshy, affable, long-suffering comic strip character holding up a picket sign that read, "Ziggys of the World Unite!"

"So wouldn't that make you a Vulcan, too?" I asked.

"Technically, yes," she replied, "though unlike Mother and Father I was born on a spaceship, and Earth is the only planet I've ever known. They, on the other hand, remember our home planet vividly."

"Have they shown you photos of it?" I asked.

"Not photos in the conventional sense," she replied. "Vulcans outgrew what humans know as photography, having developed the capacity to share memories with one another telepathically, through a phenomenon known as a mind meld."

"And you've melded minds with them?" I asked.

"Oh yes," she said, "we do it all the time. It's how I know that Vulcan is a desert planet, far lovelier than Earth, and why we can go without water for much longer than the average human, who hasn't had to adapt to such austere living conditions."

"You do know you're pregnant?" I said.

"So I'm told," she replied.

"And why you're here?"

"I'm here," she said, "as a preliminary step to aborting said pregnancy."

"That's right," I said.

Behind her sat the clinician, her highlighted Afro wagging. I didn't like being there any more than Teri did, but as a physician I believed it important for patients to understand each step of a procedure they had elected, and as I described to her the technique known as vacuum aspiration, I wasn't sure she did. Teri had, after all, claimed to have been born onboard a Vulcan spaceship, and during my brief presentation had not so much as blinked, much less registered through facial cues that she grasped what would be done to her. Her expression was blank, and I felt less in the

The Embers

presence of a teenager who had gotten herself into a bind from which her parents, pastor, and I hoped to free her than in that of a traumatized psyche so deeply buried as to be unknowable without force.

"Not every patient who opts to abort a pregnancy," I said, "can predict how she'll feel about it later," and recommended three psychiatrists who specialized in treating post-partum depression in patients who had lost unborn babies.

I wrote their names and telephone numbers on a prescription pad, and as I pulled the sheet from it, Teri said, "Don't worry about me."

"Oh yes," I said. "I forgot. You're Vulcan. Like Spock on Star Trek, you don't have emotions."

She laughed, and even it sounded mimicked, like a myna bird's imperfect replication of human speech. "That's a common misconception."

"What is?" I asked.

"That Vulcans have no emotions. We have emotions. We're simply not slaves to them, having developed highly refined methods of controlling them." She smiled at me as if with great compassion. "I understand that this is hard for you, Dr. Holcomb."

"I don't perform abortions," I said, "except—"

"I know," she said.

"How?"

"The confirmation class, remember?"

Unlike the two teenagers on whom I'd performed abortions in the past, girls whose bodies had matured early and who, from the vantage point of having gotten pregnant, spoke with authority about the pressures they'd experienced, the temptations to which they'd succumbed, and the gravity of the decisions they were making, Teri might as well have been discussing a tonsillectomy.

If I was able to hide my agitation, the clinician was not hers. "What I'd like to know," she said, "is whether that baby you're carrying is Vulcan or not."

Teri turned to her. "Of course, it's Vulcan. I'm Vulcan. I was born into a Vulcan household."

"But how many Vulcans do you know, honey," the clinician asked her, "outside of your immediate family?"

"None," Teri replied.

"So it isn't even half human?"

"Not even half."

I brought the consultation to an end by reminding Teri that the State of Minnesota required a parent's signature. Teri assured me that her father would fax the consent form to the clinic from his office and, low and behold, it was waiting for me in my mailbox, signed by the relevant party, when I returned from walking Teri back to the waiting room.

That afternoon I fired the clinician for insubordination. She hadn't worked for us long, six weeks tops, and I no longer remember her name if, indeed, I ever knew it.

"Do what you have to," she replied as she collected her things from the lab, "but that poor child was raped. By someone she knows all too well."

"We don't know that she was raped," I replied, though I knew it the same as she.

What was more, Teri knew that we knew it, for both the clinician and I had seen the flutter of panic as it came to her, what she'd admitted.

•

A few weeks later I came home from work to find my family seated at the kitchen table staring at a wrinkled flyer. September had arrived and the boys were back in school, Luke in 12th grade, Vance in 10th, and while I'd enjoyed horsing around with them all summer, Lorna had confided to me that she was ready to have the house to herself again. Luke captained the cross-country team, Vance played tight end on the Junior Varsity football squad, and from 7:30 in the morning when I dropped the boys off at school until 5:30 in the evening when the friends of theirs who owned cars brought them home, Lorna's weekdays were her own. Never one to complain, she was less high-strung once autumn came, and over the years I'd come to associate the reds and yellows of the elms, oaks, and maples, through which sunlight filtered in resplendent hues, with domestic tranquility if not bliss. Not only that, Luke had been accepted into the U.S Naval Academy in Annapolis as a midshipman, having—on his own recognizance — solicited a letter of nomination from then-U.S. Congressman Al Quie in the months before he was elected governor, and with the money I'd set aside for his college education I put a down payment on an A-frame cottage outside Hayward, Wisconsin, the self-proclaimed musky-fishing capital of the world.

The lakefront property, bordered on the north by the Chequamegon National Forest, included a dock and the previous owner's Crestliner fishing boat, rigged with a 90-horse outboard and in-dash sonar fish-finder, and at night as I fell asleep, I imagined the lunkers that would surface for my plugs, spoons, and crankbaits. The previous Sunday Lorna had cancelled our upcoming canoe trip down the Saint Croix River with your family to spend the weekend "beautifying" our new lake place, an effort to which I hoped to add a trophy that, from snout to tail, would span the length of the fireplace mantel. What made me giddier still was the distance it would put between you and me, for the get-away would mean missing a Sunday worship service for once.

Though the abortion had gone well enough, with Glen having taken off time from work to accompany his daughter to and from the clinic, afterward I felt as if I'd not only ended a human life but destroyed criminal evidence. Without DNA samples from Glen and the fetus, for which one would need a court order, there was no way to establish paternity, and from this alone I derived solace. For his part, Glen, distracted and fidgety, provided none, and I wondered what Teri had told him about her consultation. If he was guilty and knew that I knew it, I predicted he and Myrna would leave our congregation and bridge group, and though I didn't know it on the evening that Lorna, Luke, and Vance sat me down at the kitchen table to show me the notice Vance had removed from a telephone pole three doors down from our house, they already had.

The flyer had been crudely made, the lettering cut from newspaper headlines and pasted onto a page that had then been photocopied.

dR. BrUCe HoLcoMb, m.D.
YOUr NeiGhBorhOod AboRtioNISt
StOP iN foR yOUR freE ConFIDeNtIal
cOnSultATioN NO jOB toO sMAll oR ToO bIg!!!

At the bottom of the flyer were the addresses of my home and office as well as the telephone numbers where I could be reached. In the middle was an illustration, taken from an anatomy textbook, showing a baby, its eyes closed in slumber, nestled in the womb.

"Dear Lord," I said.

"They're up all over town, Dad," Vance said. "So far Luke and I have ripped down more than fifty."

"The first one I saw was five miles from here," Luke added, "on a run. We need to report this to the police."

"We will. We will," I said, enveloped by something resembling shock. I say 'resembling' because I was as calm and cognizant of what was happening around me as I was in surgery, when all eyes but the patient's were trained upon my gloved hands as they cauterized, excised, and sutured within a narrow opening. Yet I was also removed, as if observing myself from a distance, the way I, too, in surgery watched my hands, as if they, and not I, were responsible for the operation's success or failure.

"It's slander," Vance exclaimed. "You don't perform abortions."

"You're right, I don't," I said. "Not usually." It was gratifying that Vance, too, had been attentive during my sex talk.

"What do you mean, 'not usually'?" he asked.

"I've performed three that weren't medically warranted," I said, "three in thirteen years of practicing medicine."

I said it not to redeem myself, for in truth I felt about what I'd done as he seemed to, his cheeks as flushed with outrage as they were when refs overlooked an opposing team's penalties, but rather to hear what God would hear if He in his infinite compassion existed, which I doubted.

"You shouldn't have performed even one," Vance said. "That's what you said."

"That is what I said."

"Then you lied to us," he replied. "Why did you lie?"

I had no answer for him. In time, Luke said, "Give Dad a break, Vance. I'm sure he had his reasons."

"Go fuck yourself, Luke," Vance said.

"Hey!" I scolded him. "That's no way to talk to your brother."

"No, Vance, you go fuck yourself," Luke

said and slugged him in the arm.

When the boys were younger, I would wash their mouths out with soap for using less vulgar language, but they were too old for that now, and I felt as if I, at the root of their disagreement, were powerless to rectify it. Lorna's head was bowed. I did not discuss medicine with her and assumed she was as disturbed as Vance by my confession. Raised in the Methodist tradition, she had never not gone to church and, before we were married, insisted our children be raised as Methodists too. Upon first settling in Edina, she found Good Sam in the phone book, and from then on, I mouthed the prayers and hymns, took communion, and wrote checks to the church that, I assumed, were as large as any in the offering plates. If the community's affluence was reflected in the deep pockets of the congregants, many of my patients were church members, and in my more cynical moments I thought of the amount I gave to the church as my advertising budget.

Lorna looked up and said, "Let's go to The Embers," a dimly lit Twin Cities franchise that offered booth seating in a burnt umber décor and a crosshatched New York strip steak, baked potato, and wedge salad for under seven dollars. The closest was five minutes away, just off the freeway next to the Howard Johnson's. Lorna hadn't started dinner, so we four piled into the Volvo as we did on other family outings, and in this soon-to-be defunct local institution had our last supper. Lorna ate mutely, and in time, I feared, I'd hear what she thought about what I'd done, but upon our return, after we'd played back all the answering machine messages from anonymous callers informing us that I was going to Hell, after the boys had retired to their bedrooms to finish their homework amidst all the phone ringing, Lorna and I lay in bed wondering if the ringing would ever cease, for by then the answering machine had reached its storage capacity and we'd resolved not to answer the phone again.

Between rings, Lorna turned to me and told me that she knew Katie Schnegel and I were having an affair, that she'd observed me kissing Katie on the lips outside her apartment that afternoon and wanted a divorce.

"Why, Bruce?" she said. "Why?"

I could've fought to save our marriage. I could've told Lorna that Katie and I had broken up earlier that day, which we had, that the kiss we'd exchanged had been that of lovers acknowledging irreconcilable differences, which it had, and that the affair had been a one-time deal, which it hadn't, but I didn't.

The phone rang again, and I said, "Because when I'm in bed with her I feel like God."

"Then I guess 'God' doesn't live here anymore," she replied.

•

I retired from medicine a year later, my heart no longer in it. Since then, I've lived an ascetic life on Ghost Lake in the A-frame I bought in the weeks before Lorna and I divorced, and from April through October I fish for muskies. There are big ones in the lake, some thirty yards beyond the railing of my redwood deck and framed by balsams, birches, spruces, and hemlocks that form a natural arbor through which, with binoculars, I can see who's fishing the south slough. I've hauled in plenty over the years, though none as large as the one I've observed on still evenings lurking a few feet beneath my plug as I've jerked it across the surface to affect the appearance of prey. All the muskies I've caught up here I've returned to the water—the meat is palatable but packed with tiny, translucent bones that, once lodged in the throat, are difficult to extract—and I worry that the trophy fish I can see off the side of the boat, a six-foot-long, missile-shaped shadow I would mount above my fireplace if I could reel it in, remembers my landing it before, when it was younger and smaller, that something about my particular style of spin-casting reminds it of traumas past.

Lorna thinks I have too much time on my hands. At least that's what she tells me when we talk on the phone every month or so. She may be right. Always we have a lot to talk about, our sons, whose accomplishments never cease to amaze us, and our mutual friends, most of whom we met through Good Sam. Though we rarely speak of our shared past, it's never more immediate than after one of her phone calls. Then the man I am at seventy-five must reconcile himself to the man he was at forty-four, when our marriage ended and I left the church and OB-GYN clinic for good. Probably I wasn't meant for matrimony. But until one has tried it, how does one know? I tried it, loved it, and would've continued loving it if only I could've slept with any and all OR nurses who wanted to sleep with me, be they fat, thin, wide-hipped, slender-hipped, white, black, brown, or tangerine, my only stipulation being a sense of humor to compensate for my lack of one. Before Katie Schnegel there had been many, each funny in her way, and after her none.

What happens in a surgical theater stays there, and yet, for me, no sex was ever as scintillating or as satisfying as that with the nurse who had been in it with me, who'd handed me the very instrument the moment required, the particular scalpel, clamp, forceps, tenaculum, or retractor without my even having to name it, as if for the duration of the vaginal hysterectomy or the removal of the ovarian cyst she and I had read each other's minds. That's how it had been with Katie and me until she blurted out at the end of a successful, if taxing, myomectomy, as I was sewing the patient up after removing more than a dozen fibroids, "I want to have your baby, Bruce." The anesthesiologist, a burley, bearded, bear of a man, laughed through his mask, as did I as I thanked her, for her tone had been that of one delivering a punchy compliment, glibly admiring of the feat I had performed. I didn't think about it again until later that day when, lying spent beside me, she said, "I wasn't kidding earlier."

"About what?"

"Your baby." She turned onto her side on the bed so that her pigtails stuck out at angles like those of an Arrow-Thru-The-Head, a popular novelty at the time. "I'm going to have it, Bruce."

I asked Katie if she was pregnant, and she told me, "A month." She'd stopped taking the pill three months before, and for the three days she'd known the test results, she'd been too frightened to tell me.

"I'm not asking you to marry me. I'll raise the child myself. You won't be responsible to it in any way, Bruce. I just really, really want a baby. Your baby. And, I guess, your blessing."

Katie had gone rogue, and yet I felt oddly at peace, just as I did in the church sanctuary surrounded by stained glass and before me on the altar the cross rising into the airy heights of the chancel as if from a garden in full bloom. Before making love, I'd told her about the abortion I'd performed earlier in the week.

"The girl, fifteen," I said, "had likely been raped by her father, a man I play bridge with, and frankly, I don't know which to feel worse about, the taking of a human life or the destruction of criminal evidence."

"Perhaps this is something you should take up with your pastor," she replied.

"He was the one who convinced me to do it."

"Maybe you should convert to Lutheranism," she suggested.

"Myron is a good man," I said. "He was only protecting his flock, doing what he thought best."

Now, after lovemaking, Katie sat up in bed and said, "Perhaps you could think of this as

43

returning stolen goods, a life we're bringing into the world to replace the one you took."

I wasn't about to tell her about the other two abortions I'd performed for fear she'd want three kids from me instead of just the one. "Have you spoken to your doctor about options?" I asked.

"What options?" she replied.

"You know," I said. Though I didn't perform abortions, many doctors did, a D and C as effective and safe for early miscarriages as early unwanted pregnancies.

"You're kidding, right?" she said. "You have to be fucking out of your mind."

"I have to go," I said.

"You can't leave," she said.

As usual our clothes lay scattered across her bedroom floor. I pulled a dress sock up over my calf. "If you go through with this," I said, "our relationship is over."

"It's already over. You're married. I know. How convenient for you."

By the time I was back in my suit, she was waiting for me by the door in an open robe, clothed from sternum to knees except for a strip down the middle of her the width of her neck. She followed me outside onto the walkway that looked onto the parking lot and street.

"You can't be out here like that," I said. "What if someone sees you?"

"I'm letting you off the hook. The least you can do is kiss me one last time," she said, and as I did, I closed her robe and cinched it tight.

•

September is the best month up here, ask anyone. Muskies, fattening up for winter dormancy, are less discerning than at other times of the season and when striking a surface lure explode from the lake fanning their tails. Their returns to the water are just as spectacular, cannonball splashes that resound to the mottled shorelines. The air lumbers, encumbered by the smoke of burning leaves, except when the Packers are playing, and everyone holes up in front of their TVs. When Rodgers connects with Nelson in the end zone or Lacy runs the ball up the middle for a touchdown, the chambers of shotguns and rifles empty into the sky, my own among them, and the reports echo across the lake.

Though you and I went our separate ways long ago, Myron, Lorna and Bev are still in touch, and it's through Lorna that I know anything about you and of what your life consists, that you retired from the ministry more than a dozen years ago and moved with Bev to a condo in Saint Augustine, Florida. Good for you! Every July when you and she return to the Twin Cities for a week of catching up with old friends, Bev shows Lorna a stack of photos of you and her posing with your daughters, sons-in-law, and four grandchildren before landmarks in the oldest continuously occupied European-established settlement in the continental U.S.—the tourist district and its Spanish colonial boutiques and bistros, the beaches, harbor, fort, and lighthouse—and asks her to guess which one you've chosen for your Christmas card. Lorna always guesses wrong, basing her selection on the artistry of the composition—the scenery, light, and contrast of colors—rather than on the number of grandkids smiling, Bev's sole criterion.

Every year, Lorna tells me, you and Bev try to persuade her and Lincoln to buy a little place down there, a condo like yours with an ocean view or, at least, a view of a cypress-lined fairway, the idea being that if only she lived in a popular tourist destination, our boys, their wives, the six kids they have between them, and I, who unlike Lorna did not remarry, would want to gather for reunions once or twice a year like your family does. But what neither you nor Bev can seem to grasp is that no one in my family, except perhaps the son or daughter I've never met, enjoys spending time together as a family, despite how we appeared prior to my termination of Teri's pregnancy, and the onslaught of Right-to-Lifers it brought to the doorsteps of my residence and workplace, forcing me out of the house and into an apartment more quickly than either Lorna or I anticipated, even after we'd shared with Luke and Vance our decision to separate.

Imagine waking before dawn to a man or woman—it doesn't matter which—telling you through a megaphone that God loathes the sight of you, that to Him you are an abomination, that a seat between John Wayne Gacy and Josef Mengele has been reserved for you at Satan's table. The sky lightens on a peaceful assembly of between five and twenty planted at the end of your driveway, at your property line, waving signs calling you Doctor Death and poster-sized laser prints of fetuses. More protestors await you at work, among them a minister in a clerical collar quoting scripture from a soapbox. As you pull open the door of plate glass, he points a finger at you, bellows, "Your hands are red with blood!" You wonder why you should be targeted rather than your partner, Dr. Heath, who has quietly terminated dozens of healthy pregnancies at the same clinic where you have terminated exactly three. But you know why. Though you can't prove Teri is behind the flyers that reappear as quickly as they're torn down, you know she is the culprit, that she is making you pay not for the human life you took but for the secret you made her spill.

If I tried to set up an appointment with you to discuss my situation—and I did, to no avail—I no longer hold you responsible for the ruination of my career and family.

Lately I learned from Lorna of your imminent decline, your memory lapses, which, Bev tells her, are growing longer and more frequent, and of Bev's worries about having to commit you to an assisted living facility, which she believes will kill you. Probably the time to ask for an apology has passed—you're eighty-three, your life's work complete— but if I did, would you say, "I'm sorry, Bruce," or would you ask me why I chose to perform the abortions? Why, in particular, I performed the third one when I knew from performing the first two that it would violate my moral code?

"Because, Myron," I would tell you, "I placed your moral code above my own, believing a Methodist pastor closer to God."

"But you told me yourself," I can hear you saying, "that you don't believe in God, Bruce."

And you're right, Myron, I don't, which leaves me again with the unsettling feeling that I performed all three because I liked you, because I valued your friendship and didn't want to lose it, or you running to Sunny Li, the new OB-GYN in town, a church member, and a woman to boot, to ask her to do what I couldn't.

But what am I to make of your utter dismissal of me at the time I needed you most? Despite the old chestnut about doctors having god complexes, I am no god and cannot bring myself to forget. You will have the luxury of forgetting soon enough, a silver lining in your situation. Or perhaps you don't dwell on such matters. Why would you? For all our perceived closeness, I didn't know you beyond what I projected onto you, a dynamic most doctors know all too well.

Of course, all of this happened long ago, those marvelous dinners our families shared, when our kids jumped on our trampoline until they tired, then lay on it, staring at clouds or, if we were visiting you, played croquet until sundown when off they'd dash with Mason jars in search of fireflies that illuminated the ancient willow beside the creek that edged your lot. Across town from each other, you in old Edina, we in new, our homes were close enough to outdoor skating rinks that our kids could walk to them

from November to March and return for supper
so exhausted and ravenous that after dessert and
coffee, when it was time for our families to part,
we'd find all four passed out in front of the TV,
not even The Wonderful World of Disney able to
keep them awake.

At Least You'll Have Company

A padlock hung from the plum-colored door like a nose ring. It was Thanksgiving, 1982, and we were thinking of making Tulum our home for the winter, celebrating over camarones and beer, ceviche and margaritas, making a real feast of it. The lock sprang, and Mandy turned the handle—wobbly brass hinges that could've been removed with a Swiss Army knife should've been our first warning—and stepped inside of what, at first glance, had to be the wrong cabana.

Ours should've held our backpacks, stuff strewn around them like volcanic fallout, and through the wall of this one someone had punched a hole through which you could've driven a taxi.

The bamboo splinters around the opening were fangs carved into a jack-o-lantern's mouth. Mandy squinted at the number on the key and went back outside to check if it matched the one cut with sheers from a Tecate can. I squatted on the cement floor before an ingress that opened into tangled vines that swayed so benevolently in the torpid breeze it was hard to believe anyone could mean us harm.

"Robbed," Mandy said and onto the sand clanked the dyed hemp tote into which we'd tossed our snorkels, masks, and fins, Sartre's Being and Nothingness, which I thought romantic to read to her, our sodden, sandy beach towels, some fruit, and a silver belt buckle inlaid with abalone shards she'd bought for me from a beach vender.

"Not cool," I said.

Mandy's face reddened with anger I'd been on the receiving end of too many times to count. "Not only that," she said, "I know the asshole responsible. And if he isn't, by God he knows the asshole who is, probably by name." And off she went in her flip-flops, brown bikini bottom, and thin cotton halter-top embroidered with bougainvillea to harangue Ramon, the innkeeper, who earlier that afternoon had talked up the cabana we'd already decided to rent. Is it safe? we wanted to know, proud to have teased seguro from our limited lexicons. Having led us from the outdoor bar where he was refreshing shots of tequila for a pair of weathered, old chess players to one of six thatched huts bestrewn among a coconut grove a short walk from the sea, he pointed at the lock.

"Very," he said.

None of the other cabanas we'd looked at that day had locks. Now Mandy was yelling at him in mostly English, her voice quavering through the languorous palms and slicing through the early evening stillness.

"You need to return our backpacks on the double. With everything in them. Nada, and I meaning nada, missing."

In them we'd lugged a lot of gear useless to anyone living in tropical Quintana Roo. Hollofil sleeping bags. Woolen socks and sweaters. Long underwear. Things we'd needed in Alitak, site of the remote Kodiak Island seafood cannery

and freezer plant where we'd met and fallen into
a tentative, one-sided love but about which we
complained whenever we hefted our packs onto
the rooftop of yet another bus or train. That my
attraction to her was unrequited hadn't precluded our traveling together by ferry to the Alaskan
mainland, by thumb down most of the Al-Can
and Pacific Coast Highways to Tijuana, and by
national transportation to the Yucatán. Ready for
some R & R, we hoped to live off the three thou-
sand dollars apiece we'd saved through the summer and into the fall processing salmon and king
crab. In the spring we'd migrate back the way
we'd come and do it all over again. The problem was that most of what we hadn't spent was
in hundred-dollar bills hidden in secret pockets
we'd sewn between our backpacks and their detachable aluminum frames, making it possible, I
mused, that whoever had them might never discover the money they'd stolen.

"Look," Mandy said to Ramon, who followed behind her in orange Adidas shorts and
a lime green, salt-streaked Mexico 70 tank top,
a soccer ball composed of polygons silkscreened
across the front. Through the open door, at a distance of maybe a hundred feet, he glimpsed sunlight in a hovel without windows and broke into
a lope.

"!Carajo!" he muttered upon seeing the dev-
astation up close. "Not again. How am I ever to
make a living if they keep doing this to me?" He
wagged his head, but his frizzy ponytail remained
cemented in place by the humidity.

"Who are they?" Mandy wanted to know.

"Your guess is as good as mine," Ramon replied and raised his palms to the sky.

"I don't think so," Mandy said. "I think you know exactly who they are. Not only that, I think you're in cahoots with them."

"Me?" he said. "In cahoots with thieves?" He laughed as if the idea were ludicrous, but Mandy's expression indicated she was unconvinced. "But I am like you," he said. "Yes, I own El Paradiso, but I am not from here. I am from Cuernavaca. I studied rhizomes at the Autonomous University of the State of Morelos, but I was not cut out for it, and so, like you, I came to Tulum, not to stay but to consider my options."

Squatting on his haunches, he tossed a handful of sand in the air, and to the trains of ants in military step through the sea grass I wondered if the grains were mortar shells dropping around them, if their antennae could detect the tremors from the bombardment, though unfazed they continued in a network of arteries that lay splayed across the ground, the head of each lured onward by the bobbing abdomen before it.

"You think it's easy running a resort with them stealing from my guests every other day?"

"So we aren't the first to stay here robbed while at the beach?" Mandy asked, and Ramon smiled grimly.

"Sadly," he said, "you aren't the first and likely won't be the last. I take pride in the hospitality services I provide, but repairing cabanas has become a full-time job."

I sympathized with Ramon despite his obvious attraction to Mandy whom, I assumed, he would eventually hit on. But at twenty-one I looked to those five to ten years older than me for models of the kind of person I could be. If and when I found the one, Mandy, born five years before me on Long Island, would see that we were right for each other and no longer pine for Robert who, born in Iceland ten years before her, lived on Maui with his two young children and a wife he no longer loved. According to Mandy, Robert spent two weeks out of every four in the Kula Forest Reserve in a tent with an AK-47 protecting a half-acre he and a friend had planted with a hybrid strain of Sour Diesel and Sweet Tooth. Hired as a nanny by Robert's wife and fired by her a month later when she caught them screwing in their Jacuzzi, Mandy accepted an invitation to go camping with him and for the year before she left for Alaska divided her time between the apartment he kept for her in Kahului and his unique strain of hybrid weed sequestered in rain forest. There they slept during the day and worked at night, fertilizing topsoil, pinching meristems, separating males from females, harvesting bud, and drying it in a curing cellar he'd built with a Bobcat and twelve pallets of concrete blocks lowered by helicopter under cover of darkness. All I had to figure out was what I could offer her that would compare to that.

"So why tell us the place is seguro when it isn't?" Mandy asked.

"Because it's what I tell myself," Ramon

replied. "I tell myself the cabanas are safe because otherwise what am I to do? Can I in good faith tell guests the cabanas are seguro when they are not? No, to tell them they are safe I must believe they are safe. And, if you must know, I believe they have now been restored to their natural state of *seguro*."

"Because no one's staying here but us and anything of value we had is gone?"

"Just because you were robbed this afternoon," he said, "and many, many others have been robbed at *El Paradiso* before you, doesn't mean anyone will ever, necessarily, be robbed here again."

"Stop feeding us bullshit," Mandy said. "You misled us. You need to make it right."

"And how am I to do that?" Ramon asked. "How am I to make it right?"

"By giving us our money back for starters," Mandy said. "We paid you seventy U.S. dollars for the week."

On Ramon's face was a look I could've sworn was sympathy. "If I did that," he said, scratching his whiskers, "I would go bankrupt. Of course, I would like nothing more than to give you your money back. But to do that for you, I would have to do that for all the others who were robbed here before you, and if I did that, I would be penniless, without money to feed myself and my family, much less repair cabanas after robberies. So, you see, there is a reason for the policy, clearly posted in English and Spanish on the palm tree I trust you saw upon first entering the premises."

"Really?" Mandy said, her hands on her hips and her weight on one leg in a posture that preceded explosions of rage. "Really?" she said again, and again I felt sorry for Ramon, who had no idea of the seismic eruption gathering force within someone so petite and seemingly mild-mannered, but I did, and to spare us both I interceded.

"'Freedom,' according to Sartre," I said, "'is what we do with what is done to us.'"

I let them both sink their minds into that, and in time a grin widened across Ramon's face that correlated with his grasp of the great French existentialist's words.

"Right on, man," he said.

He rolled onto his buttocks, then onto his back and kicked the air with his sandaled feet. There was, I had come to understand, no telling how someone would react to the truth when presented to them simply and directly, and though Ramon's reaction surprised me, I affected nonchalance, which was easy enough with hair and a beard that covered all but my eyes, which were blue, nose, which sloped like my German forebears, and a triangular section of my forehead through which my third eye, I'd been told by an interpreter of Kirlian photography who'd picked Mandy and me up hitchhiking on her way to a Corvallis, Oregon psychic fair, radiated beams of silver light.

He pounded the earth with his fists, and from the pinched lime wedges of his eyes tears squirted. As his mouth oscillated between simper and sneer, I stood over him as I imagined an exorcist might.

At length, he returned to sitting and wiped his cheeks. "Thank you," he said. "I needed that."

Then and there he offered us a different cabana, this one with an unobstructed view of the sea and neither a door nor a lock but with a bed instead of metal hammock rings. He called it the Honeymoon Suite, though it was made of bamboo and thatched like all the others.

"It is too late to do it now," he said, "but tomorrow you must report the robbery to the Chief of Police. He may or may not be able to help you, but it is worth a try."

A little later, as the sun set behind us, infusing with pink the plovers and streams of wash that chased them from the water's edge and drew them back as if by magnetism, Ramon returned to our cabana with a six-pack of Carta Blanca, two tortas de jamón, and a jay—on the tray a bottle opener and book of matches. We invited him to join us—I thought for sure he would if only to put a move on Mandy—but he declined, said he had a bar to tend.

As I popped the caps off two of the cervezas, Mandy lit up and held the smoke in her lungs as if underwater. Her eyes, honey brown, looked as if they might burst from their sockets and we'd have to search for them in the sand beneath the hut, for this one rested on plywood stilts and there were gaps between the floor slats, and I imagined the tide carrying her eyes out to sea and the marvels she would see beneath the waves—the sharks and swordfish, the octopi and eels, the shipwrecks and bones of the drowned—and recount it all to me, perhaps for the rest of our lives.

"So much for our snowbird pipedream," I said.

"Now is not the time to figure things out," Mandy replied, and mirth rose from a place deep inside her, a wondrous place that, at moments like these, I longed to plant my flag and call home.

"All our money—poof!" I said and took a drag.

"I know," she said, "but look where we are." Before us stars reflected upon an ocean that merged with the sky, and in the light from them Mandy hung her bathing suit and blouse to air on a clothesline. She sat beside me on the bed, nude except for a necklace of conch shells, and the scents of her skin and hair mingled with those of the sea. She bit into a ham sandwich, said, "Good God this is delicious. Try yours."

I handed her the joint, took a bite of a ham sandwich, and washed it down with beer. It wasn't camerones a la diabla, it wasn't even a shrimp cocktail, but Mandy was right. It was delicious, and both of us high from the joint and tipsy from the beer, I draped my arm across her bare shoulders and, with her tucked in close to me, we drank our beers and smoked our pot and finished our tortas de jamón.

I didn't make a pass at her, having been rebuffed by her too many times for that. Instead, I did what I did whenever the desire for us to make love took hold: I imagined we already had. Doing it and not doing it, once the act was complete, differed only in the memory one had of it afterward, and I could make that up—how I'd signaled my intentions by gently biting the nape of her neck and she'd responded by guiding my hand to her breast, the nipple I'd twisted between my forefinger and thumb, the kiss I'd planted on her navel, the pulling back of her labia as her inner thighs pressed against my ears and the tip of my tongue lit upon her swollen clitoris, and through it all the somnolent lapping of the waves.

"You're doing it again, aren't you?" Mandy said, for I'd confessed to her in Tok, Alaska while we stood on the side of the road in an October blizzard that I had to cope with the sexual asceticism I inspired in her somehow. Before us stood no less than twenty other hitchhikers, all of us seasonal workers on our way back to the Lower Forty-Eight, and Mandy and I worried that it might be days, even a week, before we reached the front of the line. I told her she couldn't restrict my fantasy life, not if we were going to be platonic traveling partners, fully expecting her to say, yes, yes, she could. But she didn't—she merely nodded—and on the Greyhound bus we boarded when it stopped in Tok later that day, once we were snug in our seats with snow from our sweaters, wool pants, and winter caps puddling on the floor, she asked me to share one of my fabricated memories with her.

"Wouldn't you rather hear some Sartre?" I asked.

"I'd rather know what's going on inside

your head," she replied.

It seemed invasive, but she assured me she would hold nothing I told her against me, so I launched into my first memory of sex with her, this one at Alitak in her ramshackle dormitory room that overlooked Lazy Bay. Earlier that evening, a family of orca had thrice circled the harbor, a mother and three cubs, their arced backs like truck tires churning above and below the surface of the sea. At the end of the pier on which the cannery and freezer plant hung suspended over the water, we'd observed the spectacle with a congregation of seafood workers like ourselves and commercial fishermen glad for an hour of steady footing.

"Afterward," I whispered, for we weren't the only passengers on the bus, "on your bed, as we were remarking on how human the killer whales had seemed, what performers they were, showing off by rising in unison before us and misting us with spray, you didn't remove my hand from your hip, which only encouraged me to slip my fingers further inside your jeans, at which point you unzipped them yourself as I unzipped mine. 'Eat me out, Travis,' you said," but before I could describe for her listening pleasure the lovely, pungent, salty taste of her vagina, she laughed so infectiously the boy and girl across the aisle from us, a hippie couple on work visas from Poland, laughed as well and looked away.

"I would never say that," Mandy whispered back.

"Whose memory is it? Yours or mine?"

"It isn't a memory at all," she replied. "You totally made it up."

"Not the part about the whales," I said. "And anyway, who cares if it's how I choose to remember what didn't happen that night?"

"But a memory, even a false one, has to be believable. Otherwise, it's just a male fantasy. If I'm part of your memory, shouldn't I be able to recognize myself in it?"

"If I was Robert, what would you have said?"

"I wouldn't have said anything. He would've just done it. He wouldn't have had to be told."

"I'll remember that," I said.

She asked me to tell her another, so I reminded her of the hike we took up Twin Peaks, the northern and taller of which rose 1494 feet above the cannery and freezer plant, the roofs of which we'd painted forest green while waiting for the first tenders of the summer to arrive. From the summit you could see the strait known as Rodman's Reach and the barrier island known as Tanner Head and to the north the seven snow-capped sentinels cupping the Aleut village of Ah-kiok, from which a net-laden dory, a dark speck at the vertex of a long, white V, puttered toward an Indian seiner moored off Prior Point. It was ten-thirty on the evening of the solstice, and with the sun a split peach perched on a red tabletop that stretched into the Pacific, the shadow of the mountain on which we stood extended across Kempff Bay, and there we were at the pinnacle, our shadows a pair of needle-thin radio towers.

"We did it on the mountaintop?"

"Without a word, we both dropped trou. In no time you were straddling me there on the mountaintop, the survey marker cold against my ass crack, and even though we could see for miles in three hundred sixty degrees, it was as if we were in a sensory deprivation tank, so quiet the sound of our own panting was louder than front row seats at a Led Zep concert."

"I like that," she said.

"You like that it was a memory well told or you wished it was true?"

"Sorry, not falling for that," she said, but asked to hear another. So I told her about making love in her shower after sixteen hours of butchering salmon (me) and extracting egg sacs from the females (her) as they passed before us on the conveyor belt and finding scales in each other's pubic hair in spite of the rain jackets and bib overalls made of three-ply PVC we donned before each two-hour shift. I told her about quickies we'd enjoyed during mug-ups at ten a.m., three p.m., and, if we worked until midnight, eight p.m., and ten p.m., and the random meals skipped for another forty-five minutes of sexual congress here and there. I told her about the Sunday mornings spent leisurely coupling before processing began again at noon, about the Fourth of July, our only day off, and the new heights of pleasure found with the time to brainstorm, experiment, engage, reflect, and refine, an operation we henceforth referred to by the acronym BEERR. I told her about making love in my two-person Timberline, which we'd pitched on asphalt in front of the City of Kodiak ferry terminal the night before we set off for Mexico, pitched the next night on gravel at the end of the Homer spit, the night after that on a musk ox farm in Palmer, and just the night before beside the Chistochina River, the water and sky both so gray in the morning as we brushed our teeth and washed our faces that the snow in which we found ourselves an hour later, riding in the cab of a 1959 charcoal black Ford F-100 pick-up driven by a Matanuska River Valley farmer hauling what he claimed was the world's largest pumpkin strapped in tightly to the bed, shouldn't have surprised us. He was taking it to Fairbanks to a charity pumpkin-carving festival where, he said, Prudhoe Bay roughnecks were waiting with chainsaws to give it a mouth, nose, eyes, and ears.

"Ears?" we asked.

"You heard me," he replied.

Out the rear window of the cab all you could see was orange. He dropped us off in Tok, laughing as he said, "At least you'll have company."

"How many times have I come?" Mandy wanted to know. Somewhere down the beach a dancehall band covered Junior Murvin's single "Police & Thieves," its island rhythms, the product of a guitar, clavinet, and bongos, held aloft on night air so perfectly suited to the human body that one could dispense with clothes without fear of chill.

Back in Minneapolis, my mother and father were serving three types of pie to relatives who'd left their farms in central Wisconsin to spend the day eating, drinking, and watching televised football in our three-story Victorian on Franklin Street.

"Seven," I said, "and counting."

My eyes were closed as Mandy mounted me. I'd never been so high or felt such bliss, and this despite all we'd lost. It made me think that our priorities had been all wrong. All the money we'd worked so hard for all summer and into the fall mattered not at all. Let the thieves discover it hidden in our backpacks. I wanted for nothing.

Antivenom

In San Antonio, my father met us at the airport in his commissioned officer's uniform, brass caducei pinned to his lapels, and drove us to El Tropicano, a hotel with a lobby, gift shop, restaurant, and bar. It was happy hour, and our third-floor room overlooked the swimming pool where, below my sister Elaine and me, two women wearing bikinis under terrycloth robes sipped cocktails brought to them from a thatched hut by a waiter in a red tunic. Their laughter over conversation not meant for the ears of a six-year-old—this discernible from their hushed tones—wafted up through rattling palm fronds.

In a blue Ford Falcon rental car, my mother had driven us from Greeley to Denver where in a cafeteria before boarding our plane I bumped into a soldier's table and knocked his cup of coffee onto his lap. He was black, and I hid my face in my mother's skirt. Holding our tray of food in one hand and my sister's hand in the other, she apologized for my clumsiness, amid the chaos extracting from her purse two dollars that fluttered between nails I'd watched her file and polish the night before.

"Now, now," the officer said, standing up from his table and revealing the full extent of the stain across his jacket and slacks. "The little man meant no harm."

"Please," my mother said, "take the money. Your uniform will need to be dry-cleaned."

"You think the army can't afford its own laundry bill?" He laughed and adjusted his garrison cap. A big man whose roundness was betrayed by starched angles at his chest and shoulders, he took the tray of food from my mother and led us to an open table. "Now you and your children enjoy your lunch, ma'am," he said.

She thanked him, setting milk containers, apples, hotdogs, French fries, and vanilla puddings before Elaine and me. As we ate, I kept looking at the man as he blotted coffee from himself and his table with a napkin, then sat before his cup with the napkin stuffed in it, the animation I'd witnessed but a moment ago subsumed by gloom, the crescents beneath his eyes weighted and blue.

I thought about him later as I held my sister's hand, imagining lowering her on a rope and pulley from our balcony into the bed of anemones and flamingo flowers where, concealed by foliage, she could record the women whose conversation I strained to overhear. Inside our hotel room, my mother recounted her day to my father, who lay on his back on one of the double beds with fingers laced behind his head. She told him how well-behaved I'd been on the flight, how I'd looked after Elaine, letting her affix flag decals to their corresponding countries in my Flags of the World activity book and explaining to her that despite how springy the clouds looked from our airplane window she'd fall straight through them if she tried to jump on them like she did on her mattress at home.

"Norm likes when I . . ." one of the women said, but a breeze fluttered through the palms and I could not hear how she finished her sentence. "Of course, he does," replied the other.

My mother made no mention of the soldier on whom coffee had spilled, and while I was grateful to be spared the attention, even I could tell that her omission was meant to protect something that no longer existed if it ever had.

If only I could hear what Norm liked, I'd share it with my mother, and maybe my father would like it, too.

•

For the three weeks left in my father's basic medical officer training at Fort Sam Houston, my mother, sister, and I lived at El Tropicano, ate meals in our room and spent our days at the pool.

A week into our stay, my maternal grandmother Isadora, a diva wrapped in shawls of organza and tulle and partial to turbans from which sprays of orange hair erupted at odd angles, came to visit us with her second husband Leo, a rangy Texan from the panhandle. An oilman for most of his life, he'd retired to Los Angeles where he and Izzy had fallen "in cahoots," by which he meant they lived together in the yellow brick apartment building he managed three blocks off the Miracle Mile. Photos of them on the front steps between blazing pink azalea bushes in concrete urns abounded, she pumpkin-shaped and ethereal, he leather-skinned, silver-buckled, and gritty. "A real pair," my father called them behind their backs.

In the afternoons they were our lifeguards, and their laissez-faire approach to lifeguarding was a pleasant change from my mother's hyper-vigilance. While they relieved her to get her hair done, shop, or lie down for an hour in the after-noon, I dove for quarters Leo plucked from an avocado coin purse, and Elaine bobbed around the pool in a Type II boating vest, her blond hair and ever-reddening face a Janus set adrift on an orange raft. For hours she'd be as placid as the Buddha, alternating between herself and Cousin Itt, until a combination of hunger, thirst, sunburn, and boredom wormed its way into her cerebral cortex and she'd wail as if attacked by hornets, her mouth all quivering uvula, her eyes squeezed lemon wedges.

While I could've fished her out myself and placated her with bananas, Leo made such a big production of unsnapping the snaps of his west-ern shirt and draping it over the back of his chaise longue, unfastening his watchband and setting it on the table between whiskey sours, all the while saying, "You aren't really going to make your step-granddad get in the water, are you? You aren't really going to make old Leo perform a res-cue?" that I assumed he enjoyed our daily ritual as much as I did.

"You're a lifeguard," I'd say. "Saving lives is what you do."

"It's what young lifeguards do," he'd grumble. "Old lifeguards train young lifeguards to do the actual lifesaving."

He'd put out his Salem in the mound of butts that rose from the ashtray and, in his swim trunks, straw fedora, and aviator glasses, venture down the steps into the shallow end where Elaine's intermittent gasps promised a return to tranquility about as well as a machine gunner's pause to reload.

"Will you nab her, Leo?" Izzy would call from her chaise longue. "I can't take another second of her caterwauling."

"Your wish is my command, sweetheart mine," Leo would reply. And not until Elaine was swathed in arms tattooed with anchors would she desist in her keening.

Indeed, she'd stare up into the shade of his hat brim and giggle.

"Now will you look at that?" Leo would say as Izzy applauded, making all her many parts jiggle.

"My gallant prince."

It was as if each afternoon were choreographed and perfect. Once all of us were out of the water, Leo would wipe off the table with a napkin as Izzy shuffled a deck of playing cards, on each a color photograph of a mostly naked woman, for the ongoing game of gin rummy they'd been playing since 1963, the year they'd met and married.

With the coins I'd collected from the bottom of the pool I'd pay for Shirley Temples and a bag-a-piece of cheesy popcorn for Elaine and me. "English tea," Leo would call it, and draped in hotel towels Elaine and I would pretend we'd been kidnapped by royalty.

The day before they were to start back to California, Leo wanted to change the oil in their Bonneville, and Elaine and I were left alone with Izzy. In tan coveralls Leo placed his coin purse in her palm and, whistling "King of the Road," headed for the parking lot. But once we were in the water, nothing was the same. Izzy wouldn't leave her chaise longue, and the pennies and nickels she picked out from the quarters often wouldn't make the edge of the pool. While I was happy to climb out and throw the money in myself, I could see that I'd never collect enough for a single bag of cheesy popcorn much less the "English tea" we'd come to expect. Sensing a diminished return, my sister began to whimper before the sun reached one o'clock, and Izzy commanded me to make her stop.

"I can't make her stop, Grandma," I replied. As if to prove it I swam up beside Elaine and beneath the water yanked one of her feet, which made her cry even harder. "Besides, you're our lifeguard."

"I'm much more than your lifeguard, Buster Brown," Izzy replied. "I'm your grandma. And you're too big for your britches."

I threw a nickel into the deep end and swam after it. By the time I came up with it in my fist, Elaine's crying had become a squall. The only sanctuary beneath the water, I thought of myself as a dolphin, rising to the surface only for air, and each time I did Izzy was closer to the edge of the pool. The water mortified her, but could she not see that the only way to mollify Elaine was to confront her fear? Even as my sister's mewling made my teeth hurt, I was rooting for Izzy. Did she not want the same delight Elaine had brought to Leo's visage brought to her own? With eyes above the surface and ears below, I watched as water rippled up her gold polyester pants to the waist of her leopard print blouse. As she waded toward Elaine, her taut lips were those of a fledgling aerialist afraid to look down.

Once beside Elaine, Izzy spun her around by her life preserver, and I swam to them, not about to miss the change in my sister's demeanor that would bring about a corresponding one in my grandmother's. Maybe, I hazarded, I'd even get credit for it. But once embraced, Elaine looked up at Izzy's sunglasses—pearlescent cat eyes!—and screamed even louder.

Izzy snapped, "You stop your blubbering right now, child, before I wring your rotten neck. Is that what you want? For your poor, old grandma to wring your rotten neck? Because I will, child. Don't test me."

Izzy was hyperventilating, beside herself with fright, which in turn frightened Elaine, whose exasperated shrieks echoed off the sliding glass doors of hotel room balconies three stories up. "Here, Grandma," I said, "let me do it." I towed Elaine to the steps, unfastened the straps of her floatation device, and freed her from the constraints. Out of the pool, I peeled a banana, cut it into rounds, and placed them before her in a plastic bowl. Only then did her bleating turn to sniffles. Wrapped in towels, Elaine fell asleep in her chair.

Looking up from her word-search puzzle, Izzy whispered to me, "I ought to wring your rotten neck." Beneath her chaise longue the pond she'd brought with her from the pool was retreating from its shores, and her pants and blouse were mostly dry. By this time tomorrow she and Leo would be cruising west in their sea-green convertible, likely with the top down, while Elaine and I would again be under our mother's supervision and without any prospect of an English tea.

I asked Izzy if I could use her deck of playing cards to build a hotel. The air was still, and El Tropicano, towering above our oasis on four sides, would be a challenge to replicate.

Izzy glanced at me over her puzzle, her smile conspiratorial but inscrutable. "You want to build a hotel of cards? Not a house but a hotel?"

I nodded, and she handed me the deck, still in its original packaging, on the front a color photograph of a lady riding a stallion in just boots, chaps, and hat. If on each card a female model wore accessories in lieu of clothing, to me their worth lay in what could be built with them, and soon a rectangle of lean-tos linked apex to apex by cards lain horizontally across them rose from the tabletop. The first floor done, I began work on a second, and at the north end a third. By the time my mother had finished her errands, I'd used up all the cards but the jokers, and my replica was only three-fifths complete.

Without another deck, I could not go on.

"Will you look at your son's marvel of architecture and engineering?" Izzy exclaimed to my mother as she set down her department store shopping bags on the grass and moved a chair into the shade of our umbrella.

"Wow," she said, "that's the biggest house of cards I've ever seen."

"It isn't a house," Izzy corrected her, "it's a hotel."

"Not anymore," I corrected them both, turning the last two cards into a steeple. "Behold, a church."

By then Elaine had awakened and, jealous of attention directed at anyone but herself, pulled a card from the ground floor, and three dimensions collapsed into two on the beveled glass. I wasn't upset, proud of the concentration and steadiness of nerves with which I'd used every card in the deck, knowing from experience that a single, misdirected breath could raze an entire structure.

My mother snatched Elaine's card, glanced at it, and said to me, "Take your sister back to our room. The key is in my purse." Her tone one I'd heard before, I did as I was told until Elaine and I were through the gate and hidden by the wooden fence that surrounded the pool.

"God damn it to hell," she said to Izzy when she thought we were out of earshot. "Do you want them to grow up to be as trashy as you? As us? Is that what you want, Mom?"

How dare she talk to her own mother that way, I thought. Izzy's feelings were hurt, and I felt ashamed of myself for having forced her into the pool fully clothed.

"The cards are Leo's," Izzy conceded. "They're our rummy deck. Since we started playing with them, I've gone up a hundred games in less than a year. I think they give him a little thrill." She twittered a little laugh. "You might consider giving Jim a little thrill every once in a while."

"Mom," she said, "he's an OB-GYN. He sees more in a workweek than Leo will ever see in a raunchy deck of playing cards."

"I'm sorry, darling," said Izzy.

"Come on," I said to my sister and tugged her gently away from a bird of paradise in full blossom, thinking myself stupid for not having looked closer at pictures I wasn't likely to see again.

•

One evening we rented paddleboats, a red one for my father and Elaine and a yellow one for my mother and me. In a sunset that limned with flame each ripple and suffused with emerald the broadleafed ferns that cascaded to a bank of the San Antonio River, we raced each other to the cheers of restaurant patrons sitting beneath umbrellas—red, yellow, green, orange, and blue—that spotted the other. Cypress trees formed bridges over the water, and in their canopies, though only July, Christmas lights twinkled. Beneath the surface over which we glided, their reflections twinkled back as if proof that all things had their twins, even us.

At no time had I seen my parents happier. "Pump harder," my mother cried. "We can't let them win!"

"I'm on to you, Linda," my father called, aiming to cut in front of us and secure a victory for himself and Elaine, but my sister's feet fell short of her pedals, and four legs trumped two.

"We did it!" my mother shrilled as we high fived.

Thieves' gloves contracting in the night, bats snuffed out fireflies whose sputtering paths remained on the retina even after their lives were over. With Cokes for my sister and me and frozen margaritas for our parents, we toasted the end of my father's basic medical officer training, ten weeks in which his time had been divided between combat drills and surgery, the battlefield and the operating room. If in one arena his commanding officers had risked the lives of drafted doctors in war games that prepared them for nothing they would actually face stationed at military hospitals stateside, their orders in the other, often betraying questionable judgment, risked the lives of patients.

My father blamed it on the branch's "competing power structures," hating that his practice of obstetrics and gynecology was overseen by a podiatrist who also happened to be a decorated colonel.

"The clown's never performed a vaginal hysterectomy in his life, never removed an ovarian cyst, performed a tubal ligation, or even delivered a baby, and he feels qualified to tell me what to do?"

During the one night a week the army granted my father leave to visit us, my mother did her best to console him. "At least you're not going to Vietnam. You're two and through."

"That's if I live through this, Linda," he'd say and remind her that he was allergic to the anti-venom used to treat viper bites. During field exercises the men regularly encountered rattlesnakes, cottonmouths, and copperheads sunning on the limestone shelves over which they climbed and hidden in the grass through which they crawled, grenades detonating all around them, bullets zinging over their heads, no one sure if the ammo fired was real or not. Loaded with blanks, their own weapons were useless against a poisonous snake reared to strike, and some of the men had the fang marks in their battle fatigues to prove it.

But my father wasn't one of them, and the threat of a deadly snakebite was but a distant memory as our waitress nestled skillets of fajitas between Talavera ramekins of guacamole, salsa verde, and sour cream and tortillas kept warm in foil. "Tomorrow Fort Hood," my father said, and my mother explained to Elaine and me that the army had waitlisted us for a two-bedroom house on-base. In the meantime, she explained, we'd live in a two-bedroom apartment in Killeen.

"It may not be God's country," my father added, "but it'll be better than this."

"Who'd have thought," I said, "we'd ever

tire of hotel life?"

I hadn't—I would miss El Tropicano's endless supply of miniature boxes of Cap'n Crunch and Apple Jacks that opened into their own rectangular cereal bowls; the maids Carmela and Rose who when they changed our sheets stepped around my Hot Wheels raceway, thirty-two feet of orange track, start gate, stop gate, and daredevil loops I'd set up between the beds; and suspended on brackets from a wall of our room the Magnavox color television so much fancier than our old Zenith black and white—but perhaps I'd fallen under the spell of my parents' optimism.

Neither had seemed happy in a long time, and though I'd looked everywhere for the reason, browsing magazines and books in the hotel gift shop, watching soap operas on TV, and at the pool and in the lobby eavesdropping on couples I thought in love, language, whether spoken or in print, presented a second riddle I could not unravel.

But maybe, I thought as our parents joked and laughed and kissed in front of us, my misgivings had been for naught, and all was fine.

Nothing Has to Happen

His late model Mercedes-Benz E-Class convertible, the green finish so dark it looked black in the sunrise, broke down on I-40. He'd been twelve miles east of Amarillo, in the left lane passing a semi hauling pigs, the snouts and tagged ears sticking out between the metal rails of the stock trailer, when his car lost power. Jamming the gas pedal did nothing. Behind him another truck driver blared her air horn, braked to avoid upending him. When his hood fell even with the first semi's rear guard, he veered across the right lane onto the shoulder. His car stalled, and the two trucks between which he'd been boxed shrank to nothing on the flat expanse of Texas panhandle freeway.

This was the story Joe would tell Lorraine when she came to his campsite that evening in flip-flops and powder blue sweatpants cut off at the knees, carrying in her arms her service lapdog, a Maltese terrier named Fairbanks.

"I got here a little after noon," she explained, "had my tent all set up and pretty when this asshole in his seventies pulls up to my site and asks me if I'm camping alone. I tell him I am—big effing mistake!—and he pulls into the site right next to mine. Now I can't get rid of him." Her fingers scratched nervously around her dog's ears and under its collar. Her eyes, makeup-less, pled with him. "I know you don't know me from Adam, or I guess Eve, and I sure don't mean to be a nuisance, but the jerk glommed onto me, and now I don't know what to do." She smiled ruefully. "Guess I'm asking you to keep an eye on us."

Joe pulled the tab on a can of double white ale from a local brewery back in Albuquerque. He'd filled a cooler with them before leaving home, imagining the campsites off the interstate at which he'd sip them, the campfires beside which he'd sit and the stars that would effervesce in his mind, cleansing it of detritus. Until a year ago, he'd been an air traffic controller driven by a singular vision: mandatory retirement at age fifty-six, a pension, the chance to write. Indeed, he was on his way from New Mexico to Virginia for a weeklong writers' workshop at a former boys' camp in Millboro where he and six others would share a bit of what they'd written with one another and an instructor who'd published—not self-published—books. The problem was he'd written nothing, nothing, at least, that he could share, and he was giving himself a week to get there with the hope that his past would spread out across the horizon and the material worth writing about would appear as road signs designating notable points of interest.

Afterward, inspired by the experience and to avoid returning too quickly to a wife needing a break from his bullshit, he thought he might drive on to Chicago to console his sister, divorced after fifteen years of marriage, then to northern Minnesota where, at her ninety-year-old boyfriend's lake home on Lower Whitefish Narrows, his eighty-two-year-old mother was savoring each white-capped, resplendent day like it was her last.

Today had nearly been his. Luckily, he'd only blown a fuel pump, which had taken a mechanic all morning and most of the afternoon to replace.

"Well," Lorraine said as if dismayed by his passivity, "thanks a million."

Only then aware that she had been awaiting his reply, Joe said, "Listen, I'm sorry. I've had a rough day on the road." Moved by the sympathy he saw in the lines of her face, he told her about his near-death experience earlier that day, the empty calories he'd inhaled in the form of convenience store donuts while waiting for his car to be repaired, not knowing if his adventure would be over before it began, if he'd have to sell his beloved Benz for parts and take the bus or, worse, fly.

"Sounds like the kind of day I had last week," Lorraine said, "when my freezer stopped working and I lost a side of steer."

"Ouch," said Joe.

"I know, right?"

He sipped his beer. "You want one?" he asked. "Got a cooler full of them."

"Nah," she said. "After drinking wrecked my marriage, I had to give it up. Real bright bulb this one." She pointed a chipped nail at her gray, recently showered hair. She was cute in a hard bit way, about his age, maybe a little younger. Her eyes, a soft blue, lit up. "But hey, the dipshit harassing me doesn't need to know that. I'm going to let drop that my husband's a cop and he'll be joining me later tonight. Maybe that'll get him to lay off."

"Are you armed?" Joe asked.

Lorraine's throaty laugh charmed him. "Under any other circumstances, I would be. I'm retired law enforcement. Served fourteen years with the OCPD. Coming here was supposed to be a spiritual retreat. I told myself I was going camping by myself to regain my trust in people. Fourteen years on the force, you see some shit, some of it your own. I packed my yoga mat, hiking boots, a couple of thrillers. A sidearm felt somehow self-defeating."

When he'd first driven into Red Rock Canyon State Park, he'd been impressed by the cleft and curves of the road down into a subterranean oasis one would never suspect lay hidden beneath the surface of these western Oklahoma flatlands. As he'd set up his tent in a site shaded by caddo maples and the narrow canyon walls, in the receding daylight the yellow-green leaves popped against the orange cliffs. Perhaps, he thought, God was smiling on him after a day of car trouble. He was mildly aware of his fellow campers, particularly the old man across from him with trousers held up with suspenders fashioned out of baling twine, a mangy pit bull/Rhodesian ridgeback mix he called "Son," and a voice that carried as if projected in an amphitheater. Joe had initially assumed he and Lorraine were father and daughter, so freely did they move between each other's camp-sites. Their banter, what he could hear of it, had the easy familiarity of blood.

Returning together with water from the potable spigot by the restrooms, he'd asked her if she liked Don Williams. "The greatest country-western singer of all time," he proclaimed. She replied, "He's all right, I guess," and he launched into "It Must Be Love." "You wanna hear me preach?" he called to her. "No thanks," she said, and he bellowed, "'For I know the plans I have for thee!' declareth the Lord," then turned to his dog, into whose bowl he sloshed water from a jug. "Son, you're my congregation of one," and trumpeted, "Trust in the Lord with all thy heart, and do not rely on thy own insight. Do not be con-formed to this world, but be trans-formed by the renewal of thy mind, that thou may prove what is the will of God, what is good, acceptable, and perfect. In all ways acknowledge Him, and He will make straight thy path. Been preaching all my life, and as the Lord is my witness I am not about to stop now."

"Are you?" Lorraine asked Joe.

"Am I what?" Joe asked.

"Armed."

"Afraid not," he said, wishing he could've impressed her with his foresight.

"Lor-raine!" the old man yelled. "This fire of yers needs tending!"

"Have you told him just to leave you alone?" Joe asked.

"Sadly," Lorraine replied, "directness with

men isn't given to me."

By then, the first stars of the night had appeared in their gauntlet of sky. The tent camping area was less than half full, with someone reading by flashlight in an orange Marmot like his in the campsite to his left and two mothers in their thirties with their pre-teen sons at the group campsite near the entrance.

"I suppose my wife would say the same thing about me, but with women."

"That's funny," Lorraine said.

Joe laughed, surprised to be enjoying himself as much as he was. Beyond a matrix of limbs and brush, the old bastard was prodding her campfire with a stick, his billy goat's beard and weathered face lit by flames and burning cinders afloat in the air.

"If you want me to tell him to leave you alone, I will," Joe said, emboldened by the beer.

"That's sweet of you, but not necessary," Lorraine said. "Just keep an eye on us. That's all I'm asking."

She flicked on her flashlight, and soon the circle of light elongated and contracted as it swung over grass and gravel like a censer, Fairbanks yelping the entire way. Every campground had its problem camper, the guy who played The Allman Brothers into the wee hours of the morning, the guy whose left-out food attracted scavengers, the guy whose extreme views resounded and annoyed. But this old reprobate was different, with his crappy, black coupe hitched to a handmade trailer, his shit strewn everywhere, and not even a tent set up by nightfall. Was he planning on sleeping in his car, under the stars, or with Lorraine in her tent?

Joe washed the pot in which he'd heated a packet of Lipton soup and opened another brew. He wasn't prone to ascribing supernatural agency to natural phenomena, but perhaps his Mercedes had stalled precisely because something—God?— had wanted him there. Had it not broken down, he would've driven a lot further, maybe as far as Arkansas. As it was, he was eavesdropping on strangers whose conversation seemed to waft in the stillness and, as he'd promised, taking covert glances at them every so often.

Lorraine sat at her picnic table as the old pervert across from her undid drawstrings on a piece of cloth housing knives he told her he'd fashioned himself in his shed, held one up to the firelight, said, "Now how's that for a pig-sticker?" Joe thought of "Night of the Hunter," the 1950's horror classic starring Robert Mitchum and Shelley Winters, and the scene near the climax in which a boy and girl raft down a river to escape the pastor who'd married their mother for the money their late father had left them as an inheritance, not knowing that theirs is but a world of make-believe and no matter how swift the current, they can't outpace the menace walking calmly behind them on the bank. Were he and Lorraine the boy and girl?

As he popped open another can, Lorraine got into her SUV, swaddling Fairbanks in her arms. "I'm just going into town for a few supplies," she called.

"You'll go into town by yourself over my dead body. I'm going with you, darling, and I won't take no for an answer."

As Lorraine started up her vehicle, the decrepit charlatan started up his, and as she came to a stop in front of Joe's campsite, the black coupe proceeded down the loop with trailer in tow. It stopped, and a flashlight shone from the darkened cavity of the sedan over the roof of Lorraine's Hyundai into Joe's face. "Why didn't you come over?" she asked him, in the driver's seat with Fairbanks on her lap, the overhead light on and engine idling. "I tried to signal to you with my flashlight. Didn't you see me? I was jerking it this way and that, trying to get your attention."

The old weirdo inched across the gravel and turned toward the park entrance. "I missed it," Joe said. He hadn't seen her flashlight signals, but he had the "pig-sticker," the blade shimmering like a tapered tongue of flame. Was it then that he should've intruded on them? He was fifty-seven, in the best shape of his adult life thanks to a hypertension scare that had sent him to the gym six days a week for interval training and body-combat classes led by female vets from Kirtland Air Force Base. Surely, he could've overpowered a dissolute septuagenarian, even a knife-wielding one, but if he and Lorraine were to get any sleep at all wouldn't he have had to kill the aged prick? And how would either of them sleep after that?

"No worries," Lorraine said. "Just knowing that if I hollered you'd come running was comfort enough. But listen, I phoned my dad. Like me, he's a retired cop. Anyway, I didn't let on to him that I was scared shitless, but instead said, 'How you doin', Dad?' to which he replied, 'What's wrong, sweetheart?' See, we have a father-daughter code we speak whenever one of us is in trouble. I said, 'I'm having the nicest conversation with this sweet, sweet man over at Red Rock Canyon, you know the state campground in Hinton?' to which he replied, 'The asshole making you uncomfortable?' I said, 'Uh- huh,' and he said, 'Want me to call the cops?' and I said, 'Uh-huh.' Long story short, Hinton police will be here in about five minutes."

"You believe the guy really is up to no-good," Joe said. The thought was sobering. Evil could take residence in the campsite next to yours, the apartment, the home.

"Didn't you hear Fairbanks barking?" Lorraine said. "He only barks when he senses danger, and he isn't barking now. Look at him, calm as can be, aren't you, hon? And you didn't see the knife the old fucker showed me, about ay-long, under the auspices of his being there to protect me."

Joe didn't want to admit that he had seen it. "You were a cop," he said. "Has the old shit done anything tonight for which he could be arrested?"

"I don't think so," she said.

"So the police may not be able to do anything?"

"They may not. But it's still better to report the incident. He could have outstanding warrants."

"So he could come back?" Joe said, wondering if he should just throw everything back into his trunk and find somewhere else to spend the night. Every other exit off the Interstate boasted an Indian casino and hotel. He could probably watch an NBA playoff game in the bar.

"Oh, I fully expect him to," Lorraine replied. "But what am I supposed to do? Pack up my stuff and check into a motel? Try to find another campground at this hour? Drive back to Oklahoma City?" In her voice he detected weariness of life's obstacles. She'd been a cop after all. "Unh-unh," she said. "I came here on a spiritual retreat. I need a spiritual retreat. And I'll be goddamned if I'm going to be denied a spiritual retreat by an old fart with a knife." She laughed. "Forgive me. I don't make a habit of using the Lord's name in vain."

"You're forgiven," Joe said and went to his cooler for another beer. "You sure you don't want one?"

"What part of 'It wrecked my marriage' didn't you understand?" she said, but before he could answer, a police truck with lightbars flashing rolled into the tent camping area. As it crunched across from them over the gravel, the driver directed a spotlight onto each campsite before arriving at the one the old troll had vacated, leaving on space blankets his pots and pans and two heaps of clothes. "Gotta go," Lorraine said, put her SUV into reverse, backed up into her campsite, and turned off the engine. He hoped he'd have a chance to apologize to her. Most of the people he knew he'd known for decades.

They were couple friends, or friends from work, and first impressions weren't anything he'd had to worry about in more than three decades. But if his writing took off, maybe he would again.

He sat at his picnic table as the police vehicle rounded the cul-de-sac, high beams exposing Lorraine's blue, two-tone tent, the clothesline to which she'd pinned her bathing suit and over which she'd draped a beach towel, the collapsible camp table on which she'd set her propane stove and lantern. Leaving the headlights on, the officer got out of her pickup, and for as long as it took Joe to finish another can of beer, the two spoke, their silhouettes statues on a stage. Almost all was said too softly for him to hear or drowned out by static from the police radio. Then someone addressed him as "Sir?" and apparitions materialized out of the darkness.

"I'd like to get a written statement from you if I might." The officer was in her thirties, built like a farm league baseball player, in jeans, t-shirt, and duty belt. Lorraine stood beside her.

"I was here," Joe said. "I can confirm everything Lorraine just told you."

The cop smiled, handed him a pad of witness forms in a burnished steel case. She told him to fill out the upper part of the top form with his name, street and mailing addresses, telephone and driver's license numbers. "Then be as exact and concrete as you can about what happened," she said. "What you saw, heard, thought, felt. Use as many forms as you need. We've got reams of them back at the station."

She tried to hand him a pen, but he'd already reached for the Pilot G-2 he'd begun keeping in his breast pocket lest ideas for stories occur to him. So far none had, which didn't mean none would.

"Can we tell him?" Lorraine asked.

"Don't see why not," the cop replied.

"Get this. The guy's a serial rapist," Lorraine said, unable to contain her excitement or her wrath. "With outstanding warrants in three states. I told you, Joe."

"She's right. He's wanted on rape charges in Nebraska, Colorado, and Utah."

"Angie here ran the license plate number on his trailer. I never got the one on his car. But it was all they needed."

"We put an APB out on him, but that doesn't mean we're going to get him tonight. At night in Hinton, it's just me, and I can't stay here till morning on the off chance he returns for his effects. The guy's a Houdini, been eluding authorities for years evidently."

"Years?" Joe said, not looking up from the page he'd completed. "So, he could return?" Angie had set her flashlight on the picnic table, and across lines Joe had filled with ink traversed the pantomiming shadow of a daddy-long-legs. He brushed the spider to the ground, wanting neither to hurt it nor the distraction of its chimera.

"I doubt it," Angie said. "Fugitives like him spook easily. It's how they're able to evade the law for so long. But he could." Joe filled in a second form followed by a third and fourth. The trick to writing was to start. Once you began, it was easier to keep going. But, he wondered, did you need the fear of death to do it at all? As he started on a sixth, Angie received a call.

"All right, Susie Q," she told the dispatcher. "I'm on my way." She told Joe to keep writing, to leave his witness statement on the picnic table. The suspect, she told them, had been identified by the night clerk at Maxine's Shell.

"If something goes wrong," Lorraine said, "and for some reason you don't apprehend him, will you let us know?"

"Sure thing," Angie said, and then he and Lorraine were alone again, sitting at his picnic table in the sputtering light of a citronella candle.

She pointed to the campsite one over from his, the tent lit from within and glowing like amber. "That guy got here just after I did. He saw everything that went down between that dirty bird and me, and what did he do? He went into his tent with a book and never came out. What's he reading in there? The Grapes of Wrath?"

Joe hadn't seen him even once. "I guess not everyone's cut out to be a hero," he said, "including me. I should've done more. I should've gone over to your campsite. Deranged motherfuckers have a way of crumpling when faced with their equals."

Lorraine laughed. "So, you were freaked out by him, too. Don't tell me you weren't."

"I'm not saying I wasn't," Joe said. "But I've always been more of a watcher than a doer. For thirty-five years I was an air traffic controller in

Albuquerque, New Mexico. Thankfully, no planes crashed on my watch, but there wasn't a second on the job I didn't think one could."

"I bet," Lorraine said.

"Like you, I'm retired, but most of my adult life I've spent imagining how I'd be after a plane crash on my watch, how the deaths of so many passengers would change me. They say air travel is safer than any other mode of transportation. Statistics bear this out, and logically, I know it to be true. But for me emotionally, spiritually, it wasn't a question of if, but when. I've been more traumatized by what didn't happen to me in my life than by what did." He laughed.

"Life always surprises the bejesus out of me," Lorraine said. "In my line of work, I saw every kind of awfulness. Let's just say, mistakes were made, in some cases grievous errors, and when you kill someone, whether by accident or willful intent, it changes you. But not in any way you can predict. At least, I couldn't. But then again, I've never thought anything that ever happened to me was fated."

"You mean, like this?" Joe said.

She thought about it. "It does seem like the old codger and I were on a collision course, doesn't it?"

"And if it weren't for that sick fuck," he said, "we never would've met. We would've seen each other, maybe acknowledged each other with a wave, but we wouldn't be talking to each other like we are now."

He was in awe of her, her percipience un-

der pressure. She'd seen more enormity in her life
than he had in his, more depravity. Her sensitiv-
ity to evil was keener, and if not for her own re-
sourcefulness, she could've become just another
statistic. A lot of good he'd been to her, and here
she was treating him as if he'd been integral to
the whole enterprise of saving herself, and maybe
him, too. Romantic feelings stirred within him,
but he couldn't act on them. If he did, he'd be no
better than his one-time brother-in-law who'd
cheated on his sister, or his mother who'd cheated on his father, something not discovered until
after his father's death. At his father's funeral
he'd gone looking for the minister and in a basement Sunday school classroom found his mother
in her boyfriend's arms, the pair squeezed into
children's desks. Unbeknownst to anyone, they'd
been lovers for decades.

No, he'd raised three boys with Ellen and
couldn't be untrue to her, even if he suspected she
was as happy to be free of him for the duration of
his road trip as he was to be free of her.

"Think we'll hear from Angie?" he asked.

"If there's one thing I know, it's cops," Lorraine
replied. "If Angie's able to put the creep in a holding
cell, the rest of her nightshift will be spent on paperwork, and if she isn't, the rest of it will be spent dog-
gedly following leads. To Angie, who I suspect is a
very good cop, if we're alive, we're an afterthought."

"So, we might still be dead by morning," Joe
said with a laugh.

"Hey, at least we can say we did everything
we could," Lorraine replied and asked to spend

the night with him in his tent. "Now hear me out," she said. "It just makes sense. If the psycho comes back, who's tent is he going to attack first? Mine. I'll leave my flashlight on inside, so he thinks I'm there. Fairbanks will sleep with us in your tent—he's never without his mama—and he'll hear him even if we don't."

"I don't know," Joe said.

"It'll give us time to react. To overpower the coot."

"Unless he's carrying a gun," Joe said.

"If he's armed," Lorraine admitted, "you're right, our chances of surviving go down. But he never showed me one, and even if he's the world's greatest escape artist, he's also a braggart. If he's carrying a gun, he would've wanted me to see it."

Candlelight flickered in her pupils. For as long as he'd been with Ellen, he hadn't slept beside any other woman, and he snored, something she disingenuously described as "comforting." Now here was someone he was attracted to but barely knew, asking to snuggle with him.

"Nothing has to happen," she said and laughed as if conscious of her own innuendo, and still he wondered if she meant that something could. He'd mentioned he was married, and he wasn't hiding his hands, his gold wedding band reflecting the candlelight so that it looked like his ring finger was shackled in flame.

"But what if I want something to," he said, "and that's what scares me?"

He said it without guile, but her mouth contorted and the horror that knit her brow made him wish he'd been less forthright. It was as if a bat had passed between her visage and the moon, and then she was standing, Fairbanks cradled in her arms, so quiet Joe had forgotten the dog had lain nestled in her lap at all. Now it growled at him.

"You're right," she said. "It's one bad idea after another with me. My whole life, it's been out of the frying pan and into the fire."

"What?" he said, "No-o-o," but she was already striding over grass and gravel toward her campsite.

He followed her. "You're right. Nothing has to happen. We should share my tent, for safety's sake, in case the fiend returns."

"Stay away from me," Lorraine said, Fairbanks' barks puncturing the stillness.

He imagined running after her, tackling her onto the ground, but he wasn't a monster. It had been a long time since he'd made love to anyone. He'd practically given up on the idea, like Lorraine and drinking.

At his campsite, crickets chirped, leaves rustled, a small animal scurried in the brush—the night was alive with sound!

He sighed, reached for his pen and the witness forms, getting the words right, he sensed, more important than ever.

The Palisades

When I was six, horned toads inhabited central Texas in such numbers they seemed like consolation prizes for the snakes I sought but rarely found. Snakes were my first love, followed by lizards, turtles, and toads, but when I tired of poking into brambles with a stick, hoping vainly for the clack of fangs lodging into wood, then the tug of a viper writhing at the end of it, the markings hieroglyphs of a vanished tribe, I looked for horned toads. Unlike the exotic agoraphobics that awaited the gloaming coiled and cloistered in underground lairs and hunted prey under cover of darkness and brush, horned toads hid in plain sight, relying for survival on their scabby camouflage. If you saw a pebble covered with thorns, chances were, it was a horned toad.

In Killeen the apartment the Army had reserved for my family was in a complex called The Palisades, four limestone, single-story buildings of six units each. A crumbling parking lot separated Buildings A and B from Buildings C and D, and on the unpaved alleyways that divided the property into quadrants horned toads could be found sunning among the bleached stubble that rose from the caliche. A girl my age, June Pedrovsky, lived two doors down from us, and one day as she and I sat behind our building in a wardrobe box left behind by movers, I invited her to look for snakes. I could not know then that her pout was one I'd see again on girls and women I'd one day date and even marry.

"We probably won't find one," I said as encouragement. Inside the box and fused at the kneecaps, we were playing house, deciding where to put our Mondrian couch, recliner, and ottoman, our Danish modern table, chairs, and sideboard— furniture she'd seen in her mother's home decorating magazines. The corrugated sides of the box straitjacketed us, but for a time it was possible to see through the cardboard to a dining room, kitchen, living room, hallway, bedroom, and bath and imagine our imaginary things in them.

June was the more exacting of us. "The poster of the Folies Bergere should hang a little to the left, don't you think?" she'd say, and in my mind I'd move it until its placement met her expectations. "There," she'd say. "Perfect."

"Why snakes?" she asked.

"Because I'm going to be a world-famous herpetologist," I replied. Her hair, straight and black, blended with the duskiness of our enclosed confines, and her face, pale and planchette-shaped, was the moon reflecting through wisps of clouds and brittle tree limbs. She bit her lower lip, and I imagined my return from Rhodesia where I'd clocked the ground speed of a black mamba, Sumatra where I'd milked a branded krait, Bhutan where I'd hypnotized a king cobra, in the oven a soufflé she was baking to celebrate our reunion after months of my being away conducting field research.

"Herpetologists study reptiles," I said.

"I know what they do," she replied. "What I want to know is how you're going to become a world famous one."

"By starting young," I said.

Outside our imaginary home everything was white—the sky, the earth, the weeds that had withered in it—or muted shades in the process of blanching. I snapped a dead limb from a creosote bush and prodded about the base of a common tasajillo collared by knee-high fluffgrass. June stood behind me with a hand on the small of my back, her breath a salve on the nape of my neck, her apprehension about what we might flush from the thicket fortifying my own confidence and resolve. Into catclaw, smoke tree, kidneywood, and silk tassel I pointed the sharp end of my stick, certain a snake would strike it and out I'd drag a copperhead, diamondback, coral snake, milk snake, rat snake, or corn snake. A champion of the class Reptilia but a devotee of the order Squamata suborder Serpentes, I hoped June's awe over the snake's agility and grace, its markings as intricate as beadwork, its head bejeweled with eyes, its eyes black slits trapped in amber, would transfer to me.

But the heat and humidity were oppressive, my western shirt felt as heavy as a coat, and when no snakes took the bait, I said, "Let's just forget it." I planted my stick dejectedly into a porous mound rained on and baked to a hard crust. From it fire ants bubbled out in a red froth, then streamed as if from a lanced vein. "Oh Jesus H.

Christ," I said, aware that taking the Lord's name in vain would result in a mouth scrubbed clean with Dial were my mother to overhear me, but by then June and I were in a field that extended to an abandoned farmhouse, shed, and windmill that, nestled in the distance among black oaks, were the teeth of a jigsaw blade set on a horizon drawn with a straightedge. My mother had forbidden me from venturing to them, threatening if I did a spanking across my father's knee, pants and underwear pulled to the ankles.

"It's okay," June said. "There's no reason to be upset. Sometimes it's more fun to not find what you're looking for."

"When it comes to snakes?" I asked. I was an inch taller than her, and the floppy brim of her father's drab boonie hat, army issue, hid her penny-colored eyes.

"When it comes to anything you really want," she replied. "Haven't you ever wanted something so badly that all you could do was think about it? And then once you got it, you wished you hadn't because it was more fun to want it than have it?"

I thought about the toys I'd received on Christmases and birthdays—G.I. Joes, Rock 'em Sock 'em Robots, Matchbox Cars, a Johnny Seven grenade-launcher—and how not a day went by that I didn't miss them or imagine the Mayflower van pulling up to the house we were awaiting on-base and unloading the boxes marked with my name. Unpacking them would be as if all the birthdays and Christmases of my life had been

wrapped into one, I'd thought. But now I wondered. June didn't seem to miss any of her things,
though they, too, were in a box in a warehouse,
not to be delivered until the Pedrovskys moved
into the Fort Hood home the Army had promised
them. And while I told myself, just as my parents
were in the habit of telling each other, that our
apartment in The Palisades was temporary, that
making do without any of our possessions was
temporary, and that in a week, or two, or three
when we moved on-base and furnished our new
home just as we had our old, all would return to
normal, our lives no longer on hold, I didn't know
if I believed that either.

And like that, too inexperienced to know
that the exhilaration, elation, and selflessness
swirling between my ribs and spine would trans-
mogrify into their opposites as soon as we parted,
I fell in love with June. A fire ant bit my ankle,
another my calf, the pain that of a lit match held
to the flesh, but by then I'd glimpsed the fuzzy
veneer of antennas, legs, and thoraxes that had
turned the violet straps of June's flip-flops garnet,
and rather than swatting the ants from my own
legs I fell to my knees before hers and brushed off
the ants before any could bite her.

"Run," I said. And run she did, her black
and yellow shift an ensign I followed across the
field, dodging lotebush and prickly pear, skunk
bush and yucca, the ants that had affixed themselves to my legs napalm.

But I martyred myself, and when I caught
up to June at the barbed wire fence beyond which

stood the farmhouse, shed, and windmill, she turned to me. She took off her hat and closed her eyes, and I put my lips to hers. Our kiss lasted no longer than a nuthatch's chirp, but when her face came back into view, she was smiling.

"That was very sweet of you, my love," she said.

"Protecting you from the fire ants?" I asked.

"That," she said, "and bringing me back to the French Antilles. Ah, Saint Barth, how I've missed you."

Though with enough time I could have found Saint Barth on a map of the world, I knew it mainly as the home of the Guadalupe blind snake, grove snake, and two types of racer, the leeward and the Terre-de-Haut, but as I pressed one section of barbed wire down with my tennis shoe and the other up with my hand, creating the opening through which we passed, I gathered it was a tropical paradise, replete with turquoise coves, white sand beaches, and swimming pools that overlooked the sea.

June parted curtains and stepped onto our veranda. "Why look," she said as she picked up the skull of an animal with a leg still clamped in a spring coil trap chained to a spike, the pelt and entrails having receded from the skeleton splayed between tufts of lovegrass, "someone left us a coconut. Did you know that if you lop the top off with a machete you can drink the milk straight from the fruit?"

"Shall I perform the honors?" I asked.

"Would you?"

I slashed the air with my arm, which brought delight to June's eyes. The mandible lay beside scapula on the ground, and through the sockets in the cranium I could see on her palms where her lifelines and headlines converged below her forefingers and thumbs.

"I put two straws in it," she said. "You take the one closest to you." I pursed my lips as she pursed hers, and as we sipped from our coconut, our noses touched over yellowed molars, premolars, incisors, and canines lodged in the maxilla like bullets in a holster. No Saint Barth this, even the soil smelled of excrement, and though the air was still, the windmill's annular sail, missing all but two of its blades, creaked as it turned, the Aermotor emblem on the aluminum vane a riddled gun club target. Condoms flapped in the brush, and shell casings, liquor bottles, crushed beer cans, tarnished spoons, stained syringes, and unsheathed hypodermic needles littered the grounds. A section of the farmhouse's canted roof had collapsed, and in an upstairs room, exposed to the elements, were an upended four-poster bed and a doctor's scale. On the porch fluttered a tattered confederate flag.

I knew we shouldn't stay, but to June we were honeymooning beachcombers, and while I was as curious as she in the cowries, conches, cones, and augers the tide deposited before us, the hermit crab that waved a claw at us, the gold doubloon from the wreck of the San Miguel, I was looking for snakes. Surely here of all places they congregated en masse.

"Well, if it isn't Baron Jean Philip Lafite Rothschild III," June said, "the resort's resident iguana." Before us was plopped a horned toad. I picked him up, and he flattened like gelatin across my palm, broadening until his squat legs dangled from either side of it. "He doesn't bite," June assured me. "Baron Jean Philip eats only haricots verts imported from Champagne, France."

"Hairy Cots Verts?" I asked.

"Only the most perfect green beans on God's green Earth," June replied.

Though Jean Philip was easily the thirtieth horned toad I'd seen that day, I wanted to believe that he was special, that God had placed him in our path for a reason. His skin, like a cat's tongue, was pebbly to the touch, and as I stroked it, I held him before me as a talisman, a miner's canary, for while I knew better than to follow June into the wooden shed that gaped before us, the door listing from a mangled hinge, feathers aloft in slants of light that sifted through the roof, I was afraid to leave Saint Barth, worried that our love couldn't survive anywhere else.

Nevertheless, when my mother called me by my given name, middle initial, and surname in a tone I associated with swift, often head-spinning retribution for wrongdoing, I was relieved. She stood on the other side of the barbed wire fence in a dress covered with cherries, her face flushed in anger that would not subside until punishment was meted.

June glanced at my mother haughtily, then spoke to her as if she were trespassing on private oceanfront. "I'm afraid you're going to have to peddle your wares elsewhere, Madam. Might I suggest the public beach, popular with the hoi polloi?"

"I'm sorry," my mother replied. "What did you just say to me?"

"Nothing hotel security won't tell you. Now come along, darling," she said to me.

"June," I said, shocked that she would talk to a parent this way. When my mother pulled apart two sections of barbed wire and made to step between them, I dropped Jean Philip into my breast pocket and went to her, tugging June behind me by the wrist. I could not have her and June both walking around in sandals, what with spring coil traps and who knew what other perils hidden in the brush. It had been hard enough looking after June, over whose feet the sea washed and withdrew.

When I came to the fence with June in tow, my mother grabbed her wrist instead of mine and I felt as if I were handing over a prisoner. "Ouch," June cried as my mother yanked her between parted wires, then started back across the field before I could tell whether her dress had been ripped or her skin punctured. So quickly did my mother walk, jerking June behind her as if dragging a recalcitrant dog, that soon she and June looked like spiders entangled in mortal combat, before them the limestone bunkers to which they, and I, were returning.

I took my time getting there, and when I stepped onto the concrete stoop of Building A, my mother was just leaving the Pedrovskys' apartment. Because ours was on a corner, it had an additional window the Pedrovskys' didn't have, but except for that the two were identical, with the same beige boucle couch and lounge chairs in the living room and beige Formica table and vinyl chairs in the kitchen. But while my mother rarely left the kitchen and living room and spent her days cooking, cleaning, and browsing Redbook, June's mother rarely left the bedroom, and when she did it was only to add ice cubes to her glass. To me, she was more apparition than person, and the few times I'd looked up from June's The Gnome-Mobile coloring book under which we'd hidden a copy of her father's Playboy and I'd seen her standing before the refrigerator-freezer in a black slip, I'd thought her alluring in a way my mother could never be.

I didn't like thinking of my mother there, seeing what I had seen, and wanted to protect her from hurt I knew she'd feel if she knew how drawn to it I was. "You and your little girlfriend won't be seeing each other again," my mother said, letting the Pedrovskys' screen door slap behind her.

She was prescient. The Pedrovskys moved onto Fort Hood Army Base the following week, and we followed them there a week later, but because we were put in different villages, each with its own elementary school, my mother's prediction came true. Still, I dreamed about June, and when the moving van arrived bearing my toys, I would've given them all to needy children in

Kenya for the chance to play with her again.

The horned toad is virtually extinct today, its eggs mostly devoured by fire ants. But in those days, they were everywhere, and it seemed as if they always would be. Even so, for months I kept Baron Jean Philip in a shoebox, where he ate almost everything I set before him.

Ground School

At the crash site, we gave each other a solemn high five before the plaque, bolted to the fuselage of crumpled aluminum, that commemorated the thirteen passengers and three crew members who'd died aboard TWA Flight 260 when it flew into the side of the Sandia Mountains in 1955. Then we did an about-face, too exhausted from the climb and the September heat to search through the overgrowth for stray pieces of the instrument panel, sections of the wing and tail assembly, we'd been told we'd find if we just poked around.

Before sunrise, I'd picked my 16-year-old daughter up at her mother's house. In the car, I reminded Lili of the pact we'd made at the pizza parlor, the pinky-swear that had christened it, and gave her an out. It would be a difficult hike, I said, and many who'd attempted it had turned around before seeing any of the wreckage.

"We're doing it," she said, thumbs fluttering over her iPhone's keyboard.

"You sure?" I asked.

"Do you want me to back out?" she replied.

I wanted us to do something hard and memorable, and for that to forge into something unbreakable what I felt eroding between us day by day. Her mother and I had split before her first birthday, the financial stress of co-parenting in separate households worth it to be finally free of each other. Still, I worried as Lili grew older that she held me responsible for leaving her alone with someone whose emotional instability even I couldn't endure, but I was afraid to ask. Lili was more taciturn than I, and together we could be mistaken for mutes if not for the effort I had to remind myself to exert, to inquire about her life, her friends, her interests. Reticence was, for us both, self-protective, a way to avoid hoisting ourselves on our own petards.

But if on the way up to the crash site I was forthcoming enough about my own life to elicit from her concern about her best friend's substance abuse issues, another friend's eating disorder, yet another friend's prostituting himself to an older gay man for designer clothes and weekend Vegas getaways, on the way down we reverted to our natural state of parallel isolation, only breaking the silence to grumble about obstacles that seemed even more gratuitous and irritating than they had when we'd first encountered them. It was as if the dead had put them there themselves, either to protect the sanctity of a place where all had met their end or to add to their number with the souls of violators: a 30-foot sheer rock wall; a grade punishing to the ankles, knees, and hips; a meadow of corn lilies (a member of the death camas family) in which for a quarter mile the trail vanished and on each toxic, greenish blossom a hornet rested like the black, iridescent knob of a scepter; a dry creek bed with which the trail merged and diverged without signage; a warning scrawled on a piece of notebook paper and attached to a low-hanging alderleaf limb—RATTLESNAKE!!!—that was missing upon our return to the spot, though we'd met no other hikers.

With a little under three miles to go, we drank the last of our water. By then the trail had left the intermittent shade of the forest canopy, and our city, Albuquerque, lay before us like a mirage. It was four in the afternoon, and waves of heat danced around us, skipping from cactus to cactus. I took off my drenched t-shirt and sucked what moisture I could from it, having never felt such thirst.

"It's funny," Lili said, "how hard we had to work to get to someplace so sad."

"Or to leave it," I added.

No one knew why the crash had occurred. Some said equipment failure, others pilot error. It had been a clear morning, a routine flight to Santa Fe.

When we'd met, Lili's mother and I were living in a mostly gay beach town, and it took the better part of a decade for us to realize that being straight was all we really had in common. After not having sex for a year, Lili's mother and I had the bright idea to have her, believing she would somehow save us.

No one knew anything.

I sat down in gravel in the shade of a stunted juniper. I told Lili I just needed to catch my breath, but secretly worried I would expire before we got to the car. We could see the backs of new, multimillion dollar homes, the swimming pools sapphires amid the muted greens and browns, but for me the mile or less to them was an impenetrable barrier, and I wondered if that's what it was like to be a ghost.

B-Side

Among the first purchases my father made upon moving into our olive drab duplex on Fort Hood Army Base was a Teac turntable on a cherry wood base, a silver-faced Marantz receiver with LED lamps that turned the radio dial on the AM/FM tuner arctic blue, and a pair of Ohm speakers with eight-inch woofers and two-inch tweeters that he concealed behind the Danish teak lounge chairs on which my mother set her dieffenbachias. On a Saturday morning in the fall of 1967, I watched him remove the cellophane from Herb Alpert's Tijuana Brass's The Lonely Bull and pull the record from its sleeve, careful not to mar its waxy finish. He set it gently on the platter, rotated the tone arm until the needle hovered over the lead-in groove, and with the finger lever lowered the stylus onto spinning vinyl.

I was seven, and to me the whole process seemed like a lot of work, especially since our old Sylvania console could play one side of up to ten albums in a row, dropping each onto the one before it from where they hovered at the top of the stacking spindle like the observation decks of the Space Needle, built for the World's Fair in Seattle the year I was born. But as the hisses and pops segued into cheers from the bullring and Herb Alpert's magnificent trumpet, I imagined the creature about whom the melody had been written, there behind the closed gate of the puerta de los toriles, its head and horns lowered. Did it know, I wondered, that it would be prodded to exhaustion and that its death, all but certain, would be by a sword between the withers? Or would it enter the coliseum confused, denied clarity until the moment it collapsed, buckling at the knees?

In Chaffee Village most of the kids' fathers were drafted doctors or dentists who, like mine, worked at Darnall Army Hospital, a few minutes away by car on Tank Destroyer Boulevard. But Fort Hood, Texas was also home to the 1st and 2nd Armored Divisions, their nicknames "Old Ironsides" and "Hell on Wheels" the names of a major east-west artery, and in the other half of our duplex lived Mrs. Burnett, the wife of a lieutenant in the 198th Infantry Brigade deployed to Vietnam and the first-grade teacher I wished I had. Unlike Mrs. Le Grand, in whose first-grade class I was, whose husband, she was fond of telling us, was a decorated colonel in a command post in Germany and who when cheerful called us "the little soldiers in her battalion" but who, in her natural state of paranoid irritation, treated us as if we were plotting inmates, Mrs. Burnett was calm, trusting, young, and pretty. She said that since I wasn't one of her students I could call her Emily, and on Saturday mornings when my mother baked peanut butter drop cookies with Hershey's Kisses planted in their centers, I'd put a baker's dozen still warm from the oven on a paper plate, cover them in plastic wrap, and bring them to her as an offering.

If Emily was out running errands, I'd leave the gift on her front stoop, a mirror image of our own but with a pair of folding chairs and a wrought iron table, on the top of which decorative tiles formed an image of the sun and moon. If home, she'd holler, "Coming!" through the screen door and out she'd bring Arnold Palmers on a tray, ice cubes clinking in jelly jars, the lemonade at the bottom and the tea at the top comingling in wisps in the middle. There she'd ask me about my week, and I hers, which was how I learned that her husband Brian would return home again for a visit of indeterminate length between tours of duty.

My father sat in the living room in his flannel bathrobe—likely, he'd been called to the delivery room during the night, for only then did he sleep-in on his days off—sipping coffee from an avocado coffee cup and tapping ash from a Viceroy cigarette into an orange glazed, leaf-shaped ashtray. Never in my short life had music more ignited my imagination. From the bull awaiting its contest to the death, to soldiers dispatched to the jungles of Quang Ngai Province with orders to search and destroy, to POWs in bamboo cages submerged to their nostrils in water, each note carried me to a scene of deprivation and suffering but with, to those who survived, the promise of delights as scintillating as they were mysterious. If the government was sending troops by the thousands to Southeast Asia, it was with the song "Mexico," its wistful melody whistled to a relaxed march between refrains of boisterous horns and interludes of quiet strings, that it rewarded them upon their return. Or so in my child's brain I imagined, and by the end of Side A, I'd undergone a catharsis of operatic proportions.

My perceptivity heightened, the timer ticking on the stove, kids blasting caps with rocks on the driveways, chats chortling in the forsythias became music of its own. Beyond the far wall of my parents' bedroom, lending syncopation to it like a washboard played with spoons, box springs creaked next door. I'd forgotten about Emily.

"What about Side B?" my father called to me. In the kitchen my mother's cookies were arranged in columns on metal racks on the counters, and in jeans and a blouse she stood over the sink washing a mixing bowl. My sister Elaine, four, was baking smaller versions of her own, each with a chocolate chip at its center, in an Easy-Bake Oven, a Christmas present from Santa, in whom we both still believed.

I took a paper plate from the pantry, but before I could put a single cookie on it, my mother said, "What do you think you're doing?"

"Making Mrs. Burnett a plate of cookies?" If I called her Emily, I'd receive a lecture about the respect adults, just for being adults, were due.

"Not this Saturday you're not," my mother replied. "The poor woman hasn't seen her husband in over a year."

"Lieutenant Burnett is back?" I scratched my head. "How do you know? Did you see him?"

"I don't need to see him," she replied.

My father poured himself fresh coffee from the percolator. "Why don't you help me move the old Sylvania into your bedroom?" he said to me. "That old record-player is yours now."

"Really?" I asked. "And the records, too?"

"The records, too."

Of course, my father made me promise that I would neither touch the new stereo system nor listen to any of the new records he bought for it on the old. "Old records, old record player," he said. "New records, new record player. We don't want cross-contamination. Do we understand each other?"

I nodded. Though my bedroom was not mine alone, for I shared it with Elaine, the walnut Sylvania and the albums in the record bay would be. Soon I could listen to Johnny Horton's Greatest Hits, The First Family featuring Vaughn Meader, The Serendipity Singers Sing of Love, Lies, and Flying Festoons, the Broadway recordings of Hello, Dolly, My Fair Lady, and Fiddler on the Roof, the soundtrack recordings of Funny Girl, Doctor Zhivago, and Barefoot in the Park anytime I wanted.

"What are we waiting for?" I asked, how my mother had known that Emily's husband had returned no longer of vital concern.

My father flipped the record and to "Struttin' with Maria" turned up loud, we inched the behemoth down the hallway toward the bedrooms. But as we did, the clanging box springs only grew in volume until the ruckus couldn't be ignored.

"Are Mrs. Burnett and her husband jumping on their beds?" I asked.

"You'd think they'd know better," he replied, and I could tell by the resignation in his voice that he knew exactly what they were doing and, though I did not, no way in hell was he going to tell me.

•

Because she'd overheard 'nigger' drop from Lance Willis' lips, my mother told me that under no circumstances was I ever to use it. Chaffee Village was mostly white, but at the end of our block lived the Howards, an African American family with a boy, Darden, my age, and a girl, Jenice, a kindergartner. Usually, I walked to school with the Spenser twins, Hugh and Merle, whose father was a maxillofacial surgeon, and the whole way there they'd talk about how much better their lives would be in a year when their father had completed his service commitment and they could return to their beloved Boston. But when I was late and Hugh and Merle were already on their way to school, I'd walk the half mile up the hill to Meadows Elementary with Darden and Jenice, who rarely left their house on time and were marked tardy by their teachers nearly every day, the reason, according to Darden, how long it took their mother to do Jenice's hair.

Unlike the families of draftees with whom the neighborhood was filled, Major Howard was enlisted and career military, and Fort Hood was the only home Darden and Jenice had ever known. And yet, though they'd been there before any of us arrived and would remain after all of us were gone, I thought of them as newcomers, Darden holding Jenice's hand as he peppered me with questions about boys in the neighborhood, wanting to know what sports they played and hobbies they enjoyed, what dishes their mothers prepared for supper, how their homes were decorated. While I preferred our conversations about the present to those with Hugh and Merle about the past and future, I nonetheless found them disconcerting. The duplexes with kids living in them as open to me as ours was to them, after school more than a dozen of us flowed like an amoeba between them, snacking in the kitchen of one before watching TV in the den of another.

On one of our walks to school I told Darden about Hugh and Merle Spenser, how their mother refused to free their living room furniture from the moving company's packing materials because she didn't want it ruined in such a dusty hell hole and when you sat in shorts on a sofa still swaddled in stretch wrap the backs of your legs stuck to it. On another about Jack and Jim Kraft, the former our age and the latter two years older than us, who lived across the street from me and whose parents, horror movie buffs, had turned their living room into a shrine to Bella Lugosi and Boris Karloff and hung garlic braids over the doors to keep out vampires. On the rise overlooking our backyard lived the Halls, a Mormon family of seven, the youngest of whom, Simon, dreamed of being a fighter pilot and "bombing" enemy villages with soccer balls, Frisbees, and yo-yos so that children might experience joy even during wartime, and on yet another walk to school I told them about him.

Because I didn't want Darden and Jenice to fear us, the kid I didn't tell them about was Lance Willis, who in the middle of a game of chess had picked out a Brazil nut from the bowl on our coffee table and asked me, "Know why these here nuts are called nigger toes?" It sounded like a joke, and when I wagged my head, he said, "Because they're near impossible to crack. Get it? Black don't crack?" He handed me the nutcracker no one but my mother ever touched and, even then, only when she dusted. "Go ahead," he said. "Try to crack one. Betcha can't."

In the kitchen my mother shredded iceberg lettuce for Taco Night. "They aren't even real," I said and contended that like the fruit on the dining room table they were made of clay and decorative. In my family, if someone wanted nuts, we opened a can of Planters.

"Oh, they're real all right," Lance said, chose a walnut and cracked it in half before my eyes. He pried the meat out into his palm with the metal pick and slapped the pieces into his mouth. "See?"

One morning after telling my mother that I could not bear another day with Mrs. Le Grand, which led to an argument about everything in the military being substandard, including first grade teachers, and the sacrifices all of us, not just my father, were making to the nation, a speech by my mother so impassioned that she and I both lost track of time, I caught up with Darden and Jenice as they were turning the corner onto Wainwright Drive.

"You're so lucky," I said to Darden. "I'd trade places with you in a second."

"With me?" he replied. "Why?"

"You're in Mrs. Burnett's class."

Not since her husband had returned had Emily and I enjoyed Arnold Palmers and cookies together, and if I could no longer have her undivided attention, being her student would be the next best thing.

"If you want to know the truth," Darden grumbled, "Mrs. Burnett's not all she's cracked up to be. I'll grant you she's better than Mrs. Le Grand, but who wouldn't be? Phyllis Diller?"

We laughed, and it felt good to have garnered Darden's sympathy, especially since our entire friendship was based on the sympathy he'd garnered from me. In the two months I'd lived in Chaffee Village not once had I seen him with any of the boys he knew by name, not even during recess, and I doubted any of them knew his.

"If you don't mind," he said, "there's something I've been meaning to ask you."

"Shoot," I said.

"You've told me something about just about every boy in the neighborhood. But there's one you haven't mentioned."

Ah shit, I thought, he was going to want to hear about Lance Willis, and my mind raced for innocuous details I could assign to a kid I liked the least of any of them: that his father was an anesthesiologist, that from Beaumont, Texas, he'd traveled the shortest distance of any of us to get here, that he'd tried to convince me that rooks moved diagonally and bishops up, down, and sideways, which even I knew to be false.

"Who?" I asked.

"You."

"Me? I'm an open book," I said. Nevertheless, I told him about the old Sylvania my father and I had moved next to my bed, the albums dating back to the 50's that had come with it, and I gave him my Johnny Horton impression, "In 1814, we took a little trip, along with Colonel Jackson down the mighty Mississip," which I'd perfected in the shower. I told him about Herb Alpert's Tijuana Brass and how my father, after hearing The Lonely Bull, had bought Volume 2 and South of the Border and now owned the entire catalog. "The only problem is," I said, "I'm not allowed to play them on the Sylvania and I'm not allowed to touch my dad's new Teac turntable, so the only time I get to hear them is when we have company."

"That sounds like my dad and Otis Redding," Darden said and sang, "I'm a hawg for you, baby, I'm gonna root all around your door, I'm a dirty hawg for you, baby, and I'm gonna keep on rootin'."

"What's rootin'?" I asked.

"What's rootin'?" he parroted. By then we had only to cross 27th Street to be on school property where I pictured Mrs. Le Grand at her desk in front of the classroom smirking as she drew a fat zero across from my name in the attendance ledger. While Mrs. Burnett had no doubt noted Darden's absence, I couldn't imagine her taking any joy in it. Darden checked up and down the street for oncoming traffic, then told Jenice to cross without us as he withdrew an envelope from his pants pocket. He told her not to worry, that we'd follow her into the building soon enough, that we weren't Tom Sawyers playing hooky, and when she stopped glancing over her shoulder at us with an eyebrow arched, he handed the envelope to me. In it were black and white Polaroids, twenty-four in all, and at first I couldn't have said what was depicted in them, though it would turn out to be the same in each—black skin that reflected the lamplight, curly black pubic hair, nipples, navels, midsections connected by a shaft of veins and muscle, but as if the man and woman had been cut up and their parts rearranged, the camera so close it was hard to tell where one body ended and the other began.

"Rootin'," said Darden.

Though I still didn't know what he meant by the word, I felt as if it had been as wrong of him to share the photos with me as it was of me to look at them, and yet I didn't want to stop looking at them, believing the secrets of the universe and perhaps all of creation would be availed to me if only I looked at them long enough.

"Who are the people?" I asked.

"My mom and dad," he said. "It's what they do. Pass the camera back and forth. I haven't seen them do it, but they've got hundreds of pictures like these, the oldest dating back to before I was born."

On the envelope he pointed out the date, penned in the upper left corner, which made me wonder if my own parents had a similar stockpile and one day when I was snooping around where I shouldn't there they'd be. But I knew my parents and how they were with each other and couldn't imagine that ever happening.

"If you don't believe me, come over to the house sometime," Darden said. "I'll show them to you."

"Ok," I said, though I did believe him and knew I wouldn't. I returned the photos to the envelope and handed them back to him. After that, I was never late to school again.

•

As much as I wanted to complain to my mother about Mrs. Le Grand, I'd concluded that she was my burden to bear. An argument with my mother about her not only could not be won, it would mean leaving the house late and having to walk to school with Darden and Jenice. While I would've given anything to see the pictures he'd shown me again and in class daydreamed about the hundreds I might see if only I dared to ring his doorbell, I didn't want him or anyone else near me when I looked at them, uncertain what their effect on me would be. What was in the photos seemed private, and if by looking at them at all I was violating the privacy of his parents, by wanting to do so alone I was respecting it, even as the very thought of it made me feel like a ghost.

Mrs. Le Grand—matching shocks of gray that twisted around an auburn beehive, chin wart, bifocals perched on her beaklike nose—was a holdout, one of the last proponents of a teacher's right to use corporal punishment in the classroom, and not a day went by that she didn't make a student stand in the corner or order one into the hallway for a spanking she delivered with the Tri-Delta paddleboard she kept propped against her chalkboard. Added to her roster two weeks into the semester, I'd boosted the number of students in her class above the maximum capacity negotiated by the teachers' union, and for this reason she called me "Thirty-one."

"Thirty-one," she'd say, "stand in the corner," after a pea blown from another kid's peashooter landed in her hair. "Thirty-one," she'd say, "meet me in the hall," after she'd overheard a cussword murmured by another kid during rest time. "Thirty-one," she'd say, "go to the nurse's office," after the girl seated in front of me spun in a hundred eighty degrees to avoid vomiting on her own notebook and desk.

When I explained to Mrs. Le Grand that I was not to blame for the pea, the cussword, or the vomit, she accused me of lying. "Don't think I haven't seen your type before, Thirty-one."

One afternoon during silent reading I raised

my hand and asked to use the lavatory. "You'll wait like everyone else until the bell rings," Mrs. Le Grand replied. "And because I know you don't really have to use the lavatory, you'll stand in the corner until it does."

"But I'm not lying," I said, which made a few kids laugh.

"How do I know you aren't?" she asked.

"Because I'm not a liar."

"You mean to tell me you've never lied, not once in your whole life?" she asked, and when I couldn't tell her in all honesty that I hadn't, not once in my whole life, lied, she said, "I thought as much. Now stand in the corner."

If I'd raised my hand with urgency, once consigned to a corner with my face to walls that came together at a bulletin board to which a capital "P" was impaled with a stickpin and a window beyond which waves of heat roiled like surf over the playground, the need only worsened. Time stopped. I jumped up and down, danced a little jig, all to stave off burning only exacerbated by my clenched abdomen. One kid laughed, then another, and though I couldn't see them, I imagined the entire class looking at me, and when I saw myself as they did, dancing a little jig, I laughed, too, and my bladder opened.

"Look," said a boy in the front.

"Ew," said a girl in the back.

My pants drenched, I stood upon a small, turbulent sea. Behind me, Mrs. Le Grand drove her nails into my shoulders. "You did this to spite me, didn't you?" she said, and when I turned around to face her, she wasn't the witch I'd believed her to be but rather just another sad, angry person like a lot of people became in Fort Hood, my mother among them. "Now get out of my sight," she said. "Don't bother collecting your things."

In the schoolyard, under a blanching sun, the wetness felt cool against my thighs. As I walked home, I knew my mother would be as livid about what had happened as Mrs. Le Grand had been. "Take off your clothes and get in the shower," she said after I'd recounted the incident to her. "Now," she said as she hefted Elaine from the floor, clutched her purse and keys. "I'm going to give Mrs. Le Grand a piece of my mind she'll not soon forget."

The screen door whacked shut, and our new station wagon sparked to life. It hardly mattered that Mrs. Le Grand was the object of my mother's fury when her fury itself was so terrifying. Alone in the living room I pressed the power button on my father's stereo, removed the dust cover from the turntable, pulled from the bookshelf the apple green record on the jacket of which the most beautiful woman I had ever seen sat enveloped in whipped cream, a dollop on her head like a lifted bridal veil. It was the B- Side of Herb Alpert's latest release I wanted to hear, beginning with "Love Potion No. 9" and ending with "Lollipops and Roses." As I stripped off my clothes, dropped them in the washer, and stepped into the shower, the boozy swagger of each song transported me to a refuge where the traumas visited upon one in childhood burst into dandelion spores and, appearing in their place like a shimmering Xanadu, a world of adult pleasures awaiting discovery. Though I couldn't have said what the pleasures were exactly, they would be worth the wait, Herb Alpert's trumpet triumphantly proclaimed.

By the time my mother came home, I'd returned Whipped Cream and Other Delights to its place on the bookshelf and turned off the stereo I'd promised my father never to touch. "Your wish came true," my mother announced in the kitchen. "Mrs. Le Grand and I had words, and the principal agreed to transfer you into Mrs. Burnett's first grade class. Starting tomorrow, you'll never have to see that horrid excuse for a human being again."

My mother didn't ask why I wasn't happier to learn of this development. If she had, I wouldn't have known what to tell her, but hearing my mother use the very words I myself had used to describe Mrs. Le Grand made me feel sorry for us all.

The next day at school Mrs. Burnett greeted me with a smile and directed me to a desk next to the only one left vacant. When Darden sat down at it, as I knew he must, I whispered across the aisle to him, "Don't ask me anymore about boys in the neighborhood. If you want to be a part of us, be a part. If you don't, don't."

"Ok," he said and shrugged.

•

Who doesn't recall a first exposure to racism? This is the story of mine. We were playing whiffle ball on the street the afternoon Darden tried to make friends with us. Hugh and Merle Spenser from next door were there. Jack and Jim Kraft from across the street were there. Simon Hall and Lance Willis were there, too. There were others whose names and faces I've forgotten, for we had enough hitters to advance runners home, infielders to man the bases, and Jim who pitched regardless of who was batting. He was in third grade and tall for his age, with a mop-top like the ones boys older than him wore, and I imagine chumming with us first- and second-graders fed his superiority complex, though except for this once I don't remember his ever being cruel.

Surrounding Chaffee Village were open fields where troops trained, and from one we'd dug up flat pieces of limestone that we used as a baseball diamond. When neighbors came home at the end of their workdays, we dispersed to the sidewalks, and even Lance Willis's dad, who sported a silver MGB, could drive over our infield without scratching the undercarriage. Of course, everyone knew what had happened to me in Mrs. Le Grand's class, and while they'd teased me mercilessly for a day, all agreed she'd been the one at fault. Hugh and Merle Spencer, the only ones besides myself to have witnessed the scene firsthand, even commended me on being removed from her classroom and mused aloud, if pissing my pants was all it took, why more of her students weren't pissing theirs every chance they got.

With the plastic, oversized bat Hugh swatted a hit over Simon's head and charged to first, advancing Jack and Merle to second and third. I took a practice swing and stepped up to the plate, but something wasn't right. Clutched in Jim Kraft's hand, the ball looked heavier than the hollow, perforated plaything it was, and with the scowl on his face he might've been waiting to bowl and irritated by a slow pinsetter. When the bases were loaded, there weren't enough of us for a catcher, but sensing the presence of one, I turned around and there stood Darden.

His sister Jenice practiced backbends on the Spensers' lawn, her braids tied off in a dozen pink bows. Though Darden and I had sat side-by-side in Mrs. Burnett's class for weeks, we'd said nothing to each other since my first day.

"Hey, everyone," I said, "this here's Darden. He lives six doors down, on the corner. I told him he should join us after school, and here he is."

"We all know who he is," Jim said and left the pitcher's mound as if called to home plate by the umpire. The others mobbed behind him, though I could see from their expressions that only Jim held Darden in contempt. Even Jim's brother Jack looked more worried than perturbed.

"If Darden plays," I said, "there'll be enough of us for a catcher."

"What makes you think he's one of us?" Jim asked.

"Because he lives in Chaffee Village, the same as us," I said, surprised by courage that, once shown, fueled my belief in a principle that until then had seemed abstract and inapplicable to life as I knew it. The others stood behind Jim, and I before, and behind me stood Darden. Though Jim's strength and reach were easily twice my own, I was ready to fight Goliath, and would have if Darden didn't pushed me aside.

It was as if he'd come bearing alms. From his pants pocket he withdrew an envelope. Whether it was the same one he'd shown me or a different one, I couldn't have said, for Jim snatched it from his hand as soon as he saw it.

"Now what have we here?" Jim said, Polaroid photographs fanned out like a hand of rummy, the whiffle ball he'd been holding clacking on the street until it quit bouncing and rolled into the gutter. "You know what?" he said. "These are good. These are very good. They leave nothing to the imagination." He held each at arm's length, as if he were a purveyor of fine art and arbiter of refined taste, and Darden flashed me a withering smile. Unlike me, Jim understood the worth of what he'd been given, and Darden wanted me to know it. "You can see everything."

Jack, hoping to look at them, too, clung to his brother's forearm, but Jim only held the photos higher above our heads. When he'd inspected each, he returned them to the envelope and shoved it in his pants pocket.

"You can't keep them," Darden protested. "I only gave them to you to look at."

"Well, they're mine now," Jim said, "possession being nine tenths the law."

"What's in them?" Jack wanted to know.

"What's in them?" Jim mimicked. It was as if he'd seen, in the time he'd spent looking at the photos, how much older he was than the rest of us, and as he turned toward the tan duplex in which his mother sat in their air-conditioned living room wrapped in blankets watching Dark Shadows on TV, he was the 175-year-old vampire Barnabus Collins skulking away from a kill. Darden's eyes filled with rage, but he said nothing.

"You give them back to him, you hear," hollered Lance, but Jim kept right on walking, and as angry and filled with venom as I'd been, I felt as if my own blood had been drained.

When Words Fail

Not for the first time Dugan had broken up with me citing our "irreconcilable differences," by which he meant he was sick of delving beneath the surfaces of things and availing ourselves of a fuller, richer, more intimate life as a couple. Dreams were never just as they appeared, I thought, and in every conversation, no matter how facile or arch, was fodder for further inquiry. This I maintained and do still, although on that February night in 1988, having lost my lover, friend, model, and muse, the snow falling on a Commercial Street that was anything but and the hollow knells from waves lapping against the hulls of our Portuguese fishing fleet made me doubt myself. Were not some things—an unintended slight, an unexpected switch in his temperament, a tantalizing if infuriating bon mot—best taken at face value? Mightn't loosening up, letting more slide better serve my long- and short-term interests? At the time, nothing frightened me more than the thought of dying alone.

In the Governor Bradford year-rounders Jaycie Stevens and Conrad Hoover sat at the bar hunched over their highballs as if guarding them from each other. The art world was small, and smaller still once the tourists and even a lot of the townies cleared out after the last hurrah of New Year's, leaving behind a skeleton crew of misanthropes and loners. Back then, I was one of them, not a misanthrope or a loner but a year-rounder, and I turned to the others for the social interaction that would sustain me until the marshy soil absorbed the melt, gay pride flags unfurled again from the storefronts, and the town reemerged from its chrysalis, flexing its rainbow-colored wings.

I acknowledged Jaycie and Conrad with a nod and a tip of my woolen flat cap. Threadbare flannel shirts, ripped jeans, erupting fountains of umber hair, they would've been indistinguishable from each other if not for the scrubby goatee that clung to Conrad's angelic face like a doodle by Duchamp upon a portrait by Da Vinci. I thought of Jaycie and Conrad, not without a modicum of relish, as over-educated art school dropouts whose theories precluded their ever painting anything anyone would actually want to look at, much less buy, their pictures all about texture and depriving the viewer a focal point, but when their work was shown, as all things terrible are occasionally, I'd find them leaning into each other in a corner of the gallery and deliver some nicety, the disingenuousness of which soared past them into the ether and vanished like a jet.

"Nice work there," I might say, or "There you nailed it." I patronized them, I did, not because either was a threat, but because beneath the ratty layers of their clothes were exquisite male and female forms I would've liked to capture in oil and just the right light.

Rufus was tending bar that night. I ordered my highland single malt, two fingers of Oban spilled over a cube of ice, and as he served it to me in a smudged tumbler I'd have to wipe clean with a bar nap, the whiskers that hung over his lips like an awning quivered from the air flow.

"What?" I asked and turned on my hearing aid. If what I overheard was what got me into trouble, well then, I could always turn the damn thing off.

"Your better half?" Rufus was yelling over the karaoke machine and onstage lesbians in wooly sweaters belting out "Sisters are Doin' It for Themselves" in tone deaf impressions of Annie Lennox and Aretha Franklin. "Where is he?"

"Dugan?" I yelled back, our faces no more than a couple feet from each other. "In Lyme with his parents. Probably at the golf course cross-country skiing by moonlight, trying to convince them he's just as straight and wholesome as ever."

"He dump you again?" Rufus asked.

I nodded. "But he'll come back," I said. "He always does. It's his narcissism. He can't stand the thought of someone else in one of my pictures."

That fall I had completed a series of twenty nudes set on the dunes. They were lovely compositions, the Atlantic a vulture with outstretched wings partially hidden behind barren knolls, my subject, my lovely boy, oblivious to the hunger lying in wait. The best I turned into print runs of two hundred and sold enough by Christmas not to worry about showing the originals anywhere. When summer returned, more of the prints would sell, and in time the originals would find homes in permanent collections, or so I flattered myself, and rightly, as fate would have it.

"What's with them?" I asked Rufus over the ruckus, flicking my eyes at the dejected lovebirds seated across the corner of the bar from me, surly as punk rockers. On the stage, the lesbians were offering up a version of Fleetwood Mac's "Rhiannon" I hoped never to hear again, five of them sharing the mike for the amusement of the two sitting, flinging popcorn, and clapping like walruses.

"Don't know, don't care," Rufus replied. "I'm their bartender, not their couples' therapist. They came in here apoplectic, screaming at each other. About what, I could not care less. Now they're catatonic."

"Hmmm," I mused.

•

As fate would also have it, Dugan would not return to me, but rather I to him, once it became clear to me that he was ill and would die alone in an apartment in Alphabet City if I did not go there myself to care for him. His parents knew—they paid his rent, deposited a monthly stipend in his checking account, covered his medical bills and prescription costs—but to them he was already dead, just as I was to him.

He tolerated me as best he could. What else could he do? And I painted him again and again, not in his bed or in his wheelchair or in the bath, the places where sick he posed for me, but in the settings to which his mind returned—Camp Walt

Whitman, Mallorca's Es Calo des Moro Beach, Glen Canyon's Horseshoe Bend, Race Point—settings in which he'd known, however fleetingly, happiness.

Out of respect for his wishes, I spoke only when spoken to, and in his final weeks and days I don't think he even knew I was there.

But I was there, thinking of Jaycie and Conrad, young artists I barely knew, and how I envied them that winter night when, before I left, Jaycie sipped her drink through her straw and spewed it into Conrad's face, then Conrad sipped his and spewed it into hers, and they took turns doing this until their glasses were dry.

An Incision in the Reeds

Shortly after I turned seven, the world went dark at the edges and my face fell into my bowl of Lucky Charms. I inhaled milk, marshmallow shamrocks lodged in both nostrils, and I might've suffocated if not for my father carrying me to the couch in the living room and phoning an ambulance. All I know for sure is that when I regained consciousness, I was in Fort Hood's Darnall Army Hospital where my father practiced as a medical officer. On a gurney in a lit, white room filled with clanging steel and people barking orders at one another, I looked up at my parents as they looked down at me.

"Don't move," my father said. "If you do, you could wind up paralyzed from the neck down."

I nodded, and my father frowned. "I told you not to move."

My mother explained to me that I had been given a spinal tap. "A spinal what?" I asked.

"Tap," my father said. "The drawing of fluid from your spinal column into a syringe, sometimes called a lumbar puncture."

"The doctors had to find out what's wrong with you, honey," my mother said. "It was the only way. The good news? You're going to be ok."

"Of the types of meningitis you could have," my father explained, "it's not the worst.

Your body will fight it off on its own, but you'll have to lie still for as long as it takes your lumbar puncture to heal."

"How long will that be?"

"Three or four days."

"Three or four days?"

"To be on the safe side."

"It'll go fast," my mother assured me. "You'll see."

"Look," my father said, "comic books," and fanned a dozen in the air in front of me—The Green Lantern, Captain America, Hot Stuff, Archie.

Though he'd likely purchased them in a hurry from the hospital gift shop, I imagined him selecting each with care from the magazine rack at the PX where once, while waiting with my mother in the checkout line, I'd been stupefied by a soldier riffling through one from the X-rated shelf, on the cover of which a nude, four-breasted superhero named Hestia the Beauteous had ensnarled evil industrialists in floods, magma, tornadoes, and avalanches erupting from her four nipples.

"For when it's safe," he said.

•

In Greeley, Colorado the year before my father was drafted into the Army, a kid I knew from Vacation Bible School fell off the roof of his house and broke his neck. Why he'd been up there at all, I hadn't a clue, but after the hospital released him, ladies from the church, my mother among them, met twice a week at his home to help with his physical therapy, and one June morning I went with her.

When we got there, Joel was laid out on a gurney on the patio, and while one church lady massaged his temples, the others maneuvered his limbs, bending his legs at the hips, knees, and ankles, his arms at the shoulders, elbows, and wrists, trying, my mother had explained to me on the drive there, "to help his brain remember how his body works."

Feet shorter than the elevated bed on which he moaned, I could see little more of him than the appendages that flopped about the waists of the women cradling his calves and forearms, but I remembered him sitting in the churchyard as our pretty, teenaged counselor read to us about baby Moses being left by his mother beside the Nile in a basket of pitch and tar and how annoyed I'd been by Joel's deviated septum, overbite, and the barrage of questions with which he drove my beloved Meg to distraction, such that she slapped the picture book shut on the crabgrass and declared, "I don't know about any of you, but killing all the boys makes sense to me."

The next time I went with my mother to Joel's house, I brought my periscope, a toy made of cardboard and shaped like a Z with rectangular mirrors inserted into the joints, which enabled clandestine viewers to look around the corners of buildings without being observed and over the heads of adults blocking scenes of potential interest. As the church ladies worked on Joel, I turned the spotter's wheel until his yawning nostrils appeared in the crosshairs. He raised his head, and the pupils capping his sky-blue irises bore into my one, magnified to thrice its size, floating in a box over my mother's left shoulder.

I hadn't meant to scare him, or maybe I had, but Joel screamed as if he'd seen the eye of God.

•

In Greeley, we'd lived in a square, red brick house on a corner lot, and in the backyard next to a redwood fence that followed our property line my father had planted corn. The stalks, I knew from the previous summer, would grow until they hid the steeple of the Methodist church we attended. In the same spirit, he'd ordered a yard and a half of manure from the stockyards east of town and spent a Saturday in hip-waders spreading the hovel-sized heap over the lawn, front, back, and sides, with a pitchfork. "Ours will be the greenest grass in Greeley," he exclaimed upon returning from the clinic each evening, assuring us we'd get used to the smell.

My mother indulged him with acquiescent nods, but during the day she cursed him, always under her breath lest I understood more than I let on, for an odor that had only briefly offended the olfactory when the breeze blew from the east now assaulted all five senses without remission, the methane a battering ram to the face and head. You breathed it in and nothing tasted right afterward.

One gray day, I stood inside our screened-in porch with our boxer Duchess when a lady in mourning passed by on the sidewalk. Resentful of the rain that prevented me from playing outdoors, I whispered to Duchess, "Fuck her," pointing at the lady in black who appeared to float beyond the plain of decomposing cow shit, her veil no protection against a stench that spread through the sinuses like a poisonous tide, searing optic nerves and pushing tears from their ducts. "Fuck her, Duchess," I said. "Fuck her."

The dog leapt onto its hind legs, stubby tail wagging, front paws scraping the screens, barks sharp as rifle blasts. My mother materialized behind me. "What did you just say?" she asked.

"Fucker."

In her grip my shirt collar was a noose, my five-year-old body a stiff she yanked into the house. "We don't use that word in our home. We don't use that word anywhere."

From my mother's grumbling I gathered the woman in black had lost her son in the war. From the hall closet she produced a fresh bar of Dial, and in the bathroom, she dropped the wrapper in the wastebasket. She stood me before the sink, where above the tap and hot- and cold-water cranks her neck quivered in the mirror. Below them lay my buzz cut, blond stubble as well kept as a putting green by my father and the electric shears he produced every other Sunday after supper from a shelf in our unfinished basement.

"Where did you hear it?"

"I don't know."

"Where?"

"Don't know."

She turned on the water and held the soap in the stream. "You heard it somewhere. Where?"

I didn't know where I'd heard it, if I'd heard it from her or if I'd ever heard it before. I'd been trying to tell Duchess to sic the lady when the word bubbled up from deep inside me as if it had been there since birth and always would be and no amount of soap would ever remove it.

•

The hardest part about remaining still were the haunting visions from my past, each an unbidden conviction replete with a death sentence. Yes, I'd taken pleasure in the suffering of a kid I despised. Yes, I'd delighted in the prospect of Duchess attacking a grieving mother. Yes, I'd shot and killed a robin with a slingshot. Yes, I'd gussied myself up in my mother's clothes, makeup, and jewelry and danced around our empty house singing "Getting to Know You" as if I were Anna Leonowens in *The King and I*, as oblivious to my father canting up the walk with his fly-fishing rod and creel as she was of the King of Siam listening to her from his bed chamber.

And yes, just the week before I'd stolen a snapping turtle from its owner's back stoop, having crept on my belly beside the oak panels of his family's Pontiac Safari, which was parked in a carport identical to our own, until the white plastic pail in which the creature was housed loomed but a few feet away, at the bottom of the concrete steps that led to the kitchen. From the moment I'd first seen it, in the same white bucket strapped with bungee cords to the rear carrier of the bicycle the kid who'd found it pedaled up and down our street as if to taunt me, I knew it would be mine, and as soon as I had it in my hands, the cold scutes of its plastron at rest in my fingertips, its carapace sandpaper under my thumbs, the thing itself a football nestled between my forearms and shoulders, it was.

The sun barely risen by the time I returned to my house, I yelled to my parents to come outside and see what I'd found by the swamp that buffeted our Fort Hood neighborhood to the west.

"It was just crossing the street," I said. "I'm pretty sure it's a snapper."

I held it aloft, displaying its craggy head, its eyes inkblots caught in amber, its lips pincers. Beyond its hind legs and tail, my father, knuckling a cigarette in the hand that held his coffee, examined it through the smoke and steam.

"That's quite a specimen," he agreed.

My mother, less impressed, made a face and returned to the kitchen where silver dollar pancakes and sausages sizzled on the stovetop. Any joy they'd taken in each other they'd left behind in Colorado, and though they'd spoken to me about the baby that in months would turn us into a family of five, my mother couldn't make it through a day without crying. My father, perhaps sensing an onslaught of tears, opened the storage compartment at the far end of our carport and unearthed from it an old minnow bucket from the days when he'd fished for crappies in Wisconsin as a boy.

"Now your mother's right," he said loud enough for her to hear. "It's important that you wash your hands after touching it. You don't know where it's been or what diseases it might carry."

The snapping turtle didn't look sick, but that it could be, and that it could make others sick as well, lent gravity to my role of caretaker, and for this I loved it all the more.

"And keep your fingers away from its mouth. You don't want to lose the tip of one."

This stoked the fires of my heart, for I was in possession of a creature with the jaw strength to snap a digit off at the joint, and I imagined the awe it would inspire among kids in the neighborhood, the carrot sticks and celery stalks with which we'd provoke it, the beetles and grasshoppers we'd feed it, the toads and frogs. In it, I saw an emblem of myself: a kid who, for as long as I could remember, needed to retract into his shell, his room, to read, draw, and listen to music, if he was to play well with others. The snapping turtle and I were alike, and it was mine, and as I showed it first to the Spenser twins, Hugh and Merle, with whose family my family shared a driveway, then to Jack and Jim Kraft, brothers who lived across the street from us, I didn't think about the crime I'd committed or the lie I was perpetuating with each retelling of how it had come into my possession.

"What were you doing down by the swamp?" Hugh wanted to know.

"Looking for snappers," I replied. "What do you think I was doing?"

"But it was early, right?" Merle said. "Before sun-up?"

"At daybreak," I replied, "when living things are on the move, before they go into hiding."

"Can you show us where you found it?" Hugh asked, and I told him sure, that we'd go there on bikes the next morning at sunrise and, if God smiled on us, maybe they'd find ones of their own. Not until I'd told the story again to Jack and Jim Kraft, adding to it the armadillo I'd spotted along the way and how the snapping turtle had first appeared in the darkness as a shadow among shadows, inching across the asphalt like a shifting puddle of motor oil, did the fiction supplant the truth, and when the kid from whom I'd taken it set his bike on Jack and Jim Kraft's lawn and sauntered over to us like someone searching for his lost pet, I could look him in the eyes without flinching.

We were feeding it salami with a fork, delighting at the tings! of its beak against the tines, when he said, "Howdy!" and introduced himself as Raymond Calhoun from Florence, South Carolina. New kids were always arriving to take the place of kids who'd left, whose fathers had finished their two-year stints of duty as medical

Daniel Mueller

officers and were free to return to wherever they'd
come from or set out for somewhere new, the con-
sensus being that anywhere was better than the
pit of hell known as Fort Hood. But I liked the
place, and one of the things I liked about it most
was that all of us were the same. "Gastroenterol-
ogy," he added.

"I'm Hugh, this is Merle. Boston, Mass.
Maxillofacial Surgery."

"Jack and Jim Kraft. Eureka, California. Ra-
diology."

I told him my name, said, "Greeley, Colorado. Obstetrics and Gynecology."

Our introductions made, Raymond glanced
at me askance, as if he could see me better through
one eye than two. "If I could be any kind of doctor in the world," he said, "I'd be what your dad
is," and whistled in the way soldiers had at my
mother until her pregnancy was what they noticed about her first and the whistling ceased.

I said, "He delivers babies, big whoop,"
which was as far as my father had gotten in explaining his profession to me.

"That's half of what he does," Raymond
corrected me. "The Obstetrics part. And a mighty
admirable part it is, too. Bringing life—human
life!—into the world. But then there's the other
part, the Gynecology part. That's the part I believe I was cut out for."

Jim, two years older and a head taller than
the rest of us, laughed, and we laughed, too,
not wanting to be the butt of the joke we feared
was coming, but Raymond spared us by saying,

"Handsome snapping turtle you got there," and the Spenser twins recounted the story I'd told them, omitting the poetry with which I'd intended to quell their doubts and paring it down to its unlikely facts.

"So, you got up before sunrise," Raymond said, "with the intention of catching a snapping turtle and, low and behold, there one was, crossing the street, down by the swamp?"

"You calling one of us a liar?" Jack asked, tougher than the rest of us because of the older brother with whom he had to contend, but when it came to standing up for one another, we second graders were all for one and one for all.

"Nah." Raymond grinned. "We all know the Lord works in mysterious ways. It's just that yesterday I caught a snapper myself—I showed it to you, remember? On my bike?" he said to me. "And today it's gone. Like overnight it either grew wings or built a ladder."

Merle asked if he thought mine was his, if I could've found it after it had gotten loose. "Doubtful," he replied. "But there is one way to find out."

"What's that?" asked Hugh.

"Flip it over," Raymond said. "I wrote my initials on its underside with a blue marker. RC, same as the cola."

I braced myself for the reckoning, his initials his title of ownership, but when Jim nudged the snapper onto its shell with his tennis shoe, its neck curled like a horseshoe and mouth clamped onto a loose shoelace, its underbelly was free of human marks. I'd been wholly prepared to give the turtle back to Raymond, perhaps receiving commendation for catching it before it could return to the swamp, but he'd lied about tagging it just as I had about where I'd found it—and all, I understood, to let me know he knew I'd stolen it. Maybe he'd even seen me through his kitchen window scampering off with it.

"Told you," he said and winked at me. "Not the same snapper. But it don't matter none. There's plenty more where it came from. You just have to know how to catch 'em."

"Everybody knows how to catch 'em," Jack said. "You see 'em and you pick 'em up, careful not to get a finger bit off in the process."

Everyone snickered, including me. "I mean from the swamp itself," Raymond said. "With a hook and line. Go get your bikes, I'll show you."

And that's what we did. I put the snapper back in the minnow bucket, set it by the stoop to our kitchen, and the six of us rode on our bikes to the beige duplex at the end of Marshall Street, this so Raymond could gather his tackle. I clung to the rear of our gang so as not to be the first to turn into his driveway and thereby incriminate myself, deluding myself that as long as Raymond kept my secret, I could ignore, and maybe even forget, what I'd done under the spell of jealousy.

At the swamp, our bikes on their sides like deer asleep in the horsetails, Raymond distributed silver five-aught hooks with the solemnity of a priest, then measured out six arm-lengths of nylon kite string. He showed us how to thread the twine through the eyelet, wrap it around the shank, thread it through the loops, and tighten it into a knot that would hold against a turtle's struggle for freedom.

"You bait it like this," he said, dipped his hand into a freezer bag of viscera removed, it seemed, from animals his mother had cleaned in their kitchen, and in his slick palm lay, for all I knew, an eyeball. As he ran a hook through it, careful not to prick his finger, the membranous flesh resisted, gave, and resisted again until the barb burst from the other side like a worm from a grape. He held the baited hook aloft, then twirled the line at his side like a lariat and sent it arcing over the wound-shaped slough. Fluorescent with algae, it languished in the Highway 190 drainage ditch, and through the center of it, thirty feet away, rose the twelve-foot-high chain-linked fence topped with razor wire that surrounded Fort Hood. Raymond's bait plopped just shy of the leaves and trash trapped in it, and the splash rippled outward, jostling lily pads.

"Snappers ain't picky about their cuisine," Raymond said. "They'll eat just about anything. Now go ahead and bait up."

None of us wanted to stick our hands into entrails that lay like an incision in the reeds, but when each of us had, we spread out along the bank and tossed our lines out into the muck. Merle caught the first one. "Bring him in slow and steady," Raymond called to him. Then Jim and Jack and Hugh each caught one. A couple of the snappers were a little bigger than the one I'd stolen, a couple a little smaller, but if all were to-gether in a tank, I wouldn't have been able to tell mine from the others.

And for this I had risked my immortal soul?

•

In my hospital bed I lay motionless for one day, two days, three, terrified that if I moved at all I'd wind up paralyzed, but also terrified that by re-maining still I couldn't know for sure that I wasn't paralyzed already. My father visited before and after his hospital rounds, my mother in the late af-ternoons pregnant and toting Elaine by the hand, and I was grateful for company that, for fifteen minutes or half an hour, brought relief from the litany of indictments I brought against myself. Ex-cept when I had visitors, the nurses who fed me and changed my catheter, the doctors who called me "Sport" and "Champ," I was a spectator at my own trial, I, too, the defendant, prosecutor, judge, and jury, and as much as I wanted to proclaim my innocence, no one knew better than I what I'd done and why.

I imagined growing old without leaving my bed, my arms and legs wizening as they at-rophied, whiskers sprouting from my cheeks in adolescence Rip Van Winkling into a beard, eyes wise from what they'd gleaned through win-dows and television screens, the vicarious expe-riences of visitors, and the books they'd read to me. I prayed to God for use of my limbs even as I knew all the reasons He had for denying my request and over time I reconciled myself to my fate. If Raymond Calhoun, a boy of ten, had seen through my subterfuge, how could I escape the all-seeing eye of God?

It was then, on the afternoon of the third day, that the doctor who'd performed the lumbar puncture told me that my spine had had the time it needed to heal and it was time for me to move my arms and legs. But by then I had thought about all I would miss in life, the earth and her wonders, the world and its mysteries, and decided that I preferred being quarantined. At least then I would be protected from temptations I couldn't, at seven, even begin to fathom.

I wagged my head, and he said, "See? You're fine." He reminded me that on my nightstand lay comic books, still in their cellophane. "Grab one," he said. "You know you want to." He dangled one in front of me. "It's safe now. You have nothing to fear."

Always Funny

Dewey arrived at our father's bedside three days after my sister Kay and me. We exchanged solemn greetings, all of us in yellow Tyvek prophylactic jackets the nurses had given us to guard against airborne contagions, specifically the Methicillin-resistant Staphylococcus that had spread from a sore on the back of our father's ankle up his leg and into the rest of his body. Lying asleep in his room in the Flagstaff Medical Center's quarantine unit, our father didn't have long to live. A hospital sheet covered his lower half, but his chest and arms were bare to alleviate his fever, which overnight had produced hallucinations or visions, it was hard to say which.

I'd stayed with him the night before as over and over he'd sat up in his bed and addressed figures from his past, some I'd known and some I hadn't, all of them, I had the feeling, dead. I did my best to comfort him, with pipettes of morphine and sips of Coke, the tubes running into his forearms and swaddled loins pulled taut as prison chains, as all around us spirits stood vigil.

"Really, Dewey?" my sister said, holding in her gloved fingers a glossy blue and yellow cardboard box like a small but exquisite gift he'd brought back to her from the Australian outback, where, indeed, he'd been cast in the role of Khan's manservant in the latest Star Trek reboot. "Have you no shame?"

He didn't, which was something I admired about him and feigned among colleagues and friends who didn't know to whom the trait actually belonged. The youngest of us, Dewey had escaped the pall of guilt in which I, and then Kay, had matured into teenagers, for by the time he said his first word—"Kaka!"—our father was anchoring the nightly news and no longer gave a shit what anybody thought.

"Open it," Dewey said.

"It's a fart machine," Kay said. "I see what it is."

"Then give it to Howard," he said, "He'll appreciate it," and she handed it to me.

"You kids," said our mother, who lived for family reunions, and with the four of us together in one room her husband of fifty-eight years dying was no reason to sulk. Eventually, he'd awaken, as he'd done repeatedly the night before, and Dewey would sit with him through his night terrors. I'd done it, Kay had done it, and our mother had done it night after night for almost a month inside their home in Forest Highlands, a gated community just off the highway to Sedona, until she'd had no recourse but to call an ambulance.

This deeply upset our father, whose last wish was to die at home staring through cathedral windows at ponderosa boughs draped in snow and who told our mother as EMTs wheeled him from the house on a gurney, "You're going to be haunted by this, Glenda. Haunted."

I removed the fart machine from its flimsy packaging. From the dog-eared flaps, I concluded that my brother had opened it before me, no doubt to put in the 9-volt battery. As I held the sturdy, black, flame-resistant casing housing the single, low-fidelity speaker, the thing vibrated in my latex-covered fingers as it produced one of fifteen different fart sounds, the first like a lone note performed on a tuba, the next a pitch higher and longer, a sort of whistling, the third reedy and wet. Over and over Dewey thumbed the button on the remote control, forcing from the machine its impressive repertoire of farts. The durations and tones were what distinguished them, and I imagined reproducing one on an oboe, another on a bass viol, and yet another with a gum wrapper and comb—though none was replicable, not really. One lasted a full three seconds, beginning with a squeak and ending in a sigh. Another brought to mind a slashed tire. Some sounded involuntary, others intentional. Some conveyed embarrassment, others menace.

None of us would see fifty again, and night had fallen, and it was Dewey's turn to watch over our father, but I knew he was going to get out of it, just as he had every other responsibility from the time we were kids. When I looked at him, his cheeks were glistening. Between the yellow hood that came to a widow's peak at the bridge of his tinted aviator glasses and the surgical mask that covered his nose and mouth, his cheeks were his only visible features. Except for our father who lay with arms splayed across his sheets and head atilt on his pillow, we might've been monks, each in his cowl, come to pray before a tomb.

The Way They Do in Movies

In anticipation of astronauts stepping from their lunar module onto the Sea of Tranquility and ground that might, some thought, swallow them whole, Dr. Hidalgo, an OB-GYN like my father but, unlike him, a bachelor who drove a Byzantine blue 1963 Porsche 911, set up his RV-8 Dynascope in his front yard. It was manufactured by Criterion Corporation in Hartford, Connecticut, the ad for the RV-6 in the backs of my Classics Illustrated comic books—The War of the Worlds by H. G. Wells, 20,000 Leagues Under the Sea by Jules Verne, The Man in the Iron Mask by Alexandre Dumas—I'd often pondered over, wondering how anybody could afford its $194.95 price tag.

Dr. Hidalgo's telescope was even stronger, and more expensive, its solid white optical tube as thick as a kettledrum affixed by ring clamps to a counter-weighted dual axis motor mounted on an expandable aluminum tripod. It was state of the art, an amateur stargazer's dream, and as Dr. Hidalgo alternated between fiddling with the azimuth adjustment knobs and peering through the finderscope, adults and children alike congregated around him for the chance to look through the eyepiece at the crescent moon just appearing in the twilit sky.

To celebrate the Apollo 11 moon landing, our neighborhood on Fort Hood Army Base had thrown a block party, and beside me, our elbows touching, stood Virginia Nettle, her sun-streaked hair falling to the shoulder straps of her orange shift. She'd been in the same second grade class as me, and that morning after church I'd pedaled my gold Stingray, a five-speed with a stick shift between the banana seat and handlebars, the mile and a half from our olive-green duplex on Marshall Street to her brown one on Fisher Avenue, crossing Tank Destroyer Boulevard on the way. What would happen when I got there I hadn't a clue, but I'd biked past her house enough times hoping vainly for a glimpse of her to know I had to do something, even if disrespecting the geographical parameters my parents had set for me could result in a spanking across my father's knee.

The carport was empty when I arrived, but I waited across the street until her parents and she returned in their church clothes and I greeted them on the drive. "Mr. and Mrs. Nettle," I said, having recited the words I would say to them in my head on the way there, "Virginia and I were both in Mrs. McIntyre's second grade class last year, and I'm here to invite her to a block party my neighborhood is throwing to celebrate the Apollo Eleven moon landing."

With the hair-trigger temper of one used to quashing irritations, Virginia's father spun on wingtips that glinted in the sun. "That's Sergeant First Class to you," he replied, a corner of a mouth not given to mirth rising in wry jest only once I'd saluted him. Next to him, Virginia's mother's effusiveness disarmed me. "Well, aren't you just the sweetest thing," she said, and with the hand not holding the bakery container drew my face to her mounded torso. Though my mother had been pregnant most of the previous year, I didn't know until then how firm the stretched flesh could become, but as my nose pressed against her dress, tulip patterned and smelling of bergamot, I worried she'd break it and I'd have to tell my parents yet another story they wouldn't believe however fast I clung to it.

Inside, grace was said, our "Amen" in perfect unison. Then Virginia reached for a glazed cruller and her mother swatted her wrist. "Guests first," Mrs. Nettle said, and though I would've liked the cruller myself, I chose a long john with maple frosting. The house was identical to ours, with a dining room and living room off the kitchen, and I found it strange that for a meal consisting of donuts and coffee we sat at the dining room table, each of us with a plate, utensils, and coffee cup and saucer, when we could as easily have eaten at the smaller table in the kitchen. But I made sure to lay my napkin across my lap, and when I did Mrs. Nettle complimented me on my manners.

Sergeant Nettle wanted to know in which village our neighborhood was, and when I told him Chaffee, he asked, "Your dad medical?"

Chaffee was where most of Darnall Army Hospital's medical personnel were housed. I nodded. "He's an OB-GYN."

Mrs. Nettle perked up. "What did you say your name was, sweetie?" When I told her, she swooned. "Your father's my doctor." Sergeant Nettle rolled his eyes. "Oh, come on, Ray, don't be a sourpuss," she said, slapping the back of his shaved head with her open palm, but when she turned to me, her eyes were shiny and wet. "He's just so, so wonderful, you know? Your father?" She daubed them with her napkin, and in her set jaw I saw Virginia's likeness. "I mean, it's hard to find a doctor . . . one specializing in women's health concerns . . . who both knows what he's doing and how to make a patient feel good about herself. OB-GYNs like your father are as rare as hens' teeth."

This wasn't the first time I'd heard this— Mrs. Burnett, my first-grade teacher, who lived in the other half of our duplex and whose own baby had been born a month before my brother, had told me that I had to be the luckiest boy alive to have a father who understood women so well— nor would it be the last. But as awkward as it was to hear his virtues extolled in an area I knew next-to-nothing about, I was smart enough to accept accolades on his behalf, aware that I could only profit from them.

"Why thank you, ma'am," I said. "I'm sure he'll be thrilled to know you think so highly of him."

"Oh no, you can't tell him," Mrs. Nettle replied. "That would be . . . too weird."

"Ok then," I said. "I won't tell him. But I'm sure he'd be thrilled if I did."

"Oh, I don't know," she said. "You decide. I'm big as a barn. I don't know what I think anymore." She took a bite of a Bismark and cherry filling spewed from it in a glob across her bosom. "Look at me, I'm a mess."

"Ginny?" said Sergeant Nettle, commandeering the conversation. "Would you like to go to your friend's block party?"

Virginia nodded, and my heart rose in triumph. I was Sir Lancelot and she my Queen Guinevere. I was Wilfred of Ivanhoe and she my Lady Rowena. As Virginia changed out of her Mary Janes and into her Keds, I was David Balfour and she my Catriona MacGregor Drummond. At Sergeant Nettle's request I wrote down my address and phone number on a sheet of paper and handed it to him. "You take good care of her, you hear?" he said, and I told him I would, glad these many years later I didn't kneel.

"Come on!" Virginia hollered from the street, already on her bike. "Let's go!" As I caught up to her on mine, her dress fanned out into tailfins as her hair streamed behind her. Soon we were riding side by side, and I told her about Dr. Hidalgo, his blue 1963 Porsche 911, how parked in his drive it made everything around it spin, and how he'd agreed to set up his RV-8 so that everyone in the neighborhood could look through it at the Sea of Tranquility where the Apollo 11 lunar module would shortly land and Neil Armstrong and Buzz Aldrin would later set foot.

"Dr. Hidalgo's cool," I told her. "He and my dad are both OB-GYNs at Darnall, both majors, but somehow he gets away with wearing his hair a little longer—I don't know how—and when he comes over for dinner, he always brings a date and never the same one twice. Mostly they're nurses, but once he brought a teacher."

"So, he's a playboy," Virginia said.

"Funny, that's exactly what my mom called him one night when I overheard my parents talking."

"And you think he's cool?"

From the dimple that cupped the upturned corner of her mouth, I gathered she did not. "Cooler than my dad," I said. "But not cooler than yours."

"The man you met," she said, "back at the house, isn't my dad. My dad, my real dad, is dead."

I told her I was sorry for her loss. "How did he die," I asked, "if you don't mind my asking?"

"On the ground," she replied, "fighting."

When I returned to the house with Virginia in tow, my mother and father stood in front of our new color Magnavox with Lieutenant Colonel Hall and his wife who, with their six kids, lived at the top of the crumbling hill of dirt that linked our two backyards. On the screen flickered a black and white still of craters against a backdrop of infinite space. Eagle had landed, according to Walter Cronkite's voice. On the dining room floor, my five-year-old sister Elaine sat cross-legged before my diapered brother Gus, not yet one, trying to interest him in blocks that had been mine before either of theirs. She'd place one in the willowy stubs that were his fingers—"That's the letter A. The color red. The number one."—where his dull blue eyes would examine it before he launched it a foot like something he'd coughed up. She'd hand him another—"That's the letter F. The color green. The number six."—Elaine's assiduity even then that of Sisyphus. Beyond the sliding glass doors, flames soared from the three-legged Martian otherwise known as our barbecue grill, and on the sideboard my parents had erected a cityscape of liquors, liqueurs, and mixers, my favorite the towering yellow spire of Galliano.

So transfixed were the adults by the Apollo 11 moon landing news coverage, Virginia and I were, for all extents and purposes, invisible. I led her through the living room and down the hall into the bedroom I shared with my sister, and no one said a word to us. There I showed her my collections of Matchbox cars, placing in her palm an exact replica of Dr. Hidalgo's blue Porsche 911, G.I. Joes, Classics Illustrated comic books. At the time, I owned about twenty, all but one of which I'd ordered through the mail, and rustled through Kidnapped by Robert Louis Stevenson to the page at the back with the order form listing the titles by volume number. Having saved the best for last, I produced from my closet the box containing my Thingmaker oven, bottles of Plastigoop, and metal molds, and when I lifted the lid and unveiled the components, each custom fitted to an indenture in the block of Styrofoam, Virginia's eyes widened.

"Creepy Crawlers," she said as if what had been revealed were the answer to all her dreams, as they had been to mine on Christmas morning.

"And look," I said, "glow-in-the-dark Plastigoop." On the floor was a braided rug on which we sat Indian-style before my prized possession. I plugged the metal oven's electrical cord into a wall socket, and while we waited for the Thingmaker to heat to 360 degrees, which was just one of the reasons the toy was unpopular with parents and consumer groups, we squeezed Nite Glo liquid from plastic dispensers into cavities shaped like spiders, centipedes, worms, scorpions, lizards, beetles, and snakes. When waves of heat undulated over the Thingmaker, we set the metal mold into the recess on the top of it, using the safety tongs as specified in the instructions.

"God, I love the smell of Creepy Crawlers when they're cooking," Virginia said, closed her eyelids, and inhaled the vapors, her face that of one waiting to be kissed.

My mother worried that the fumes were toxic. "Are you sure you don't want me to open a window?" I said. My mother would not have even asked.

"No," Virginia said, her voice dreamy, "I love the fumes."

"I love them, too," I said, and breathed until my nostrils tingled with the greasy redolence of oxidizing polyvinyl. For us it was an elixir that only improved our productivity, for no sooner had I pried baked Creepy Crawlers from their mold with the included stickpin than Virginia had refilled it with squirts of Plastigoop, and as soon as I took one mold out of the Thingmaker, Virginia put another one in.

"God, we're good," she said, and when all the Plastigoop was spent, the products of our labor in column formation by specie on the rug, we lay on our backs in euphoric exhaustion. "Have you ever smoked a cigarette?" she asked.

"Apparently when I was two, I ate cigarette butts out of an ashtray," I replied, "and had to have my stomach pumped. But in answer to your question, no, I've never actually smoked a cigarette. Have you?"

"No," she said. "But I'd sort of like to now. We could pass it back and forth, the way they do in movies."

I was intrigued by the idea—my father smoked Viceroys—but said, "Come on," and sat upright. "I have an idea." This wasn't something I had planned, but only seemed natural considering that all the Creepy Crawlers we'd made glowed in the dark. "We'll scatter our creations all over the backyard. They'll charge in the sunlight, and when the sun goes down, they'll glow so brightly the astronauts will see them from space."

"You think so?" she asked.

"It's worth a try," I said, and we took our Creepy Crawlers out the back door stuffed in our pockets and dribbling from our clutches.

The block party was in full swing, and men from the neighborhood, all holding cans of Schlitz or Hamm's, huddled around my father as he flipped and basted chicken while the women, most in floppy hats and sunglasses, sat together in lawn chairs, each with a Mai Tai, Harvey Wallbanger, or Old Fashioned. One thing I could say about my neighborhood: though most of the men had been drafted from private practice or straight from medical school, and none of them relished spending two years in Fort Hood, Texas, none complained about it publicly. That was reserved for the privacy of the home, and if at times I'd wondered what held my own family together through it all, the atmosphere had improved now that my father had nearly completed his service commitment and we were moving to Minnesota by summer's end.

The strange thing was, though my mother had stopped cursing and crying during the day and my father no longer came home in the evenings incensed by the incompetence and pomposity of medical officers higher ranking than himself, I already missed Fort Hood, the tarantulas that pranced like blind spots across the parched lawns, the fluorescent millipedes as wide as combs that squeezed up through the bathtub drains, the pair of coral snakes I'd found entangled in a discarded Burger Chef bag, and the diamondback that moved so mirage-like through the brush in which I played I doubted my own eyes until they fell upon the rattle dragged behind it like an awkward piece of luggage, the reticulated segments rows of baby teeth already tobacco stained.

As Virginia and I covered my family's own parched lawn as methodically as planters sowing seed, dropping a spider here, a beetle there, I already missed her, too. When we were through, I asked her if she was hungry, and she said, "Starved," so we went across the street to the Winfreys for helpings of Mrs. Winfrey's Frito pie, then zigzagged up and down the block, dining as we went. Every home was open to us, and because I'd eaten supper at least once in most of them, I could recommend what was best at each, whether it was Mrs. DeBusk's lime Jell-O with quartered canned pears suspended in it or Mrs. Spurlock's peach cobbler with its crisp lard crust or Mrs. Trickey's meatloaf, which she made with A-1 Steak Sauce instead of ketchup.

Fed and full, we played kick-the-can with some of the neighborhood kids, all of whom Virginia knew from school and who flashed each other impressed, if quizzical, glances when she punched me in the arm or booted me in the shin. These, we all knew, were displays of affection, as clear to everyone as a French kiss, and I was thrilled that she never left my side, even when we were hiding from It, which was what we were doing when Dr. Hidalgo emerged from his house with his magnificent telescope.

In Bermuda shorts and paisley knee socks, he looked as if he were carrying a sousaphone, with the mount resting on his shoulder and the dew cap the bell from which a countermarch might grumble. "Game over!" I called to everyone from our cover behind the Grandlunds' oleander bush, and when they saw what we saw they materialized from their havens like creatures entranced. Adults, too, were drawn to the spectacle, some with kids' arms wrapped around their foreheads and transistor radios glued to their ears, for by then the moon had appeared as a wisp of itself, barely there, but astronauts were on it, and the truth seemed impossible to grasp.

As we joined the crowd, Virginia was laughing. When I asked her why, she whispered in my ear, "Dr. Hidalgo isn't a playboy."

"No?" I whispered back.

"He's with a different woman every time he comes to your house for dinner because no woman will date him more than once."

Though I knew what she said was true, I pointed between the assembled at his Porsche. "What about his car?" I asked, but even it seemed duller than it had the last time I'd looked at it, as if the sun had seared some of the luster from it.

"Eh," she said. "I stand with my mom. Your dad's cooler."

"But how do you know? You didn't even meet him?"

"I saw him with the other men. When we were in your backyard. They were all listening to him with bated breath."

"And what was he talking about?" I asked.

"A patient, a golf ball. That's all I heard, but it was enough to totally convince me."

"There," Dr. Hidalgo proclaimed, "she's all lined up and ready for public viewing," as if the moon were an actress or model and he somehow responsible for how she looked that evening. He'd been born and raised in Argentina, and affectations I'd once thought women had to find charming struck me in Virginia's presence as unfortunate, if forgivable. Clearly, he was enjoying the attention, and taking joy in the anticipation each of us felt as we awaited our turns to peer through the eyepiece at a moon that would appear, he kept telling us, sixty times closer to Earth than it really was.

"Do you know what a telescope is?" he'd ask each mother and, before she could answer, say, "Nothing but a scientific means of connecting two heavenly bodies. The moon is a heavenly body and so, my dear, are you."

When it was our turn, I said to Virginia, "You go first," praying he'd refrain from the smarm for as long as it took her to see the moon in the 8-inch aperture, and he did.

"Wow," she said. "That was amazing. Have a look."

As I put my eye to the lens, Virginia placed her hand on the small of my back, and what appeared in the night sky as a slender crescent flat as a clipped fingernail appeared in the Dynascope as an orb, a sphere. You could see its curves, its craters, its lit and shaded edges. I'd looked through Dr. Hidalgo's telescope before and seen the moon when it was full, but on those occasions no people had been on it, and as I looked at it now, I kept thinking that although it was in space, it was also in Virginia's mind—she had, after all, just looked at it—and I imagined what else I might find if I dared to venture even further into the darkness.

I didn't want our day to end, though soon my mother would be calling me to come inside and get ready for bed. I asked Virginia if her mother and stepfather were expecting her shortly.

It was too dark for her to ride all the way back to her house alone, and I'd expected all along that Sergeant Nettle would eventually come to get her, her bicycle fitting easily into the back of his Country Squire. It was why, I thought, I'd written down my address and phone number for him.

So, I was surprised when Virginia replied with absolute certainty, "No one's coming to get me."

I didn't understand. "Do your mom and stepdad think you're sleeping over?" I asked.

"They aren't thinking about me at all," she replied. "They have too many other worries."

"My parents can drive you home," I said. "I'll go inside and explain the situation to them. It'll be easy."

"Please," she pleaded, "don't ask your parents to drive me home." She clung to my arm, and even as we walked down my street past windows lit by televisions, in every home someone I knew, the drag was tremendous and unexpected, and I wanted the day to end.

But I didn't know how to end it, so for a time we sat at the picnic table in my backyard. All the neighbors had returned to their homes, and the Creepy Crawlers we'd sown pulsed in tiers of greenish light, faint as the bioluminescent plankton that made the oceans sparkle at night, and in my mind, we were already much, much older.

His Future Birthplace

At the Dalton Gang's Hideout in Meade, Kansas, they met Marc, a brawny gentleman in his sixties with a Meade County Historical Society nametag pinned to his vest, a black boss-of-the-plains set back from his leathery forehead, and a salt-and-pepper soup-strainer that buffeted his chin like the dual exhausts did the padded seat on the Electra Glide parked below on the street, the pearl of its fuel tank and fenders glinting through the foliage. The bike had to belong to him. The only other visitors were an Asian family of four with two young children in khaki shorts and windbreakers madly advancing slides through View-Masters, as if at a single tourist attraction they'd discovered portals to them all.

To the west, storm clouds billowed over the prairie. "This your first visit to the Hideout," Marc asked, "where brothers Grat, Emmet, and Bob lived with their sister Eva and her husband John Whipple off and on during the late 80's and early 90's, really up until the Great Attempted Coffeeville Bank Raid of October 5th, 1892, evading U.S. marshals by fleeing through the tunnel that connects the house to the very barn where you have the supreme good fortune to stand today?"

It was the year 2000, the internet still in its infancy, and as Drew remembers it, he was at an age when time was just beginning to speed up.

"It's his," Jen said in a way that could've been meaner given the anger she'd displayed toward him on the street after he'd led her there on their Sportsters, wanting to see the effect on her of returning to a place she'd visited with Fleming, recently deceased, having eaten asphalt on his way home to Albuquerque from Creed, Colorado and a motorcycle rally at which he'd been invited to preach. "I was here in '94 or '95, though it could've been '93. I swear it's as if my brain's been pureed in a blender."

"You have a colorful way of expressing yourself, sweetheart," Marc said. "I like to think of the changes that occur to our temporal perspectives as a byproduct of the higher wisdom attained through the aging process, but perhaps that's just me." He peered down at her through the half-moons of his bifocals, never once glancing at Drew standing beside her holding her hand, and grinned.

"You might find this hard to believe, but I remember you, darling. You were here with your father, a big, silent fellow, very likeable, bought one of every postcard we keep in stock."

To give her a better idea of how many that was, Marc gave the counter-display a spin, and grasslands at sunset, jackalopes, smallmouth bass enlarged to the size of fishing boats, bedrooms, dining rooms, and parlors dripping in Victorian décor, even the two- headed Holstein calf encased in glass a few feet away creaked on a wire stand.

"He wasn't my father," Jen said, "though you're forgiven for thinking so. We were married."

Marc's eyes widened as his pupils fixed on her. She disdained men her own age and younger, of the opinion that they hadn't lived enough to hold the attention of an old soul like her. In her late twenties she'd married Fleming, then in his fifties, and Drew, now in his fifties and a mere fifteen years her senior, liked that none of his cultural touchstones were lost on her. Indeed, at forty-two, Drew had to admit, she was the more mature of them, if not in looks, in bearing. She had remained steadfastly Catholic, refusing to relinquish the transubstantiation of bread and wine into the body and blood of Christ, the splendor of the rituals, and the absolution attained through the sacrament of reconciliation.

"Your consort then," Marc said. "His name was Fleming, am I right? Corey Fleming."

"Half the time even I can't remember his full name, and I was married to him. Everyone just called him Fleming."

"Am I to take it he passed on?"

"About three weeks ago. His memorial service was in Albuquerque. It was very well attended. People loved him."

"My condolences. Though I only met the man once, I feel as if he and I were friends. Or could've been. And if that's the impression he left on me, I can only imagine the loss experienced by those who knew him well. How'd it happen, if you don't mind my asking?"

Jen sucked back a sigh. "He was riding his bike in the Rockies and spun out on a curve. He might've survived if he weren't instantly hit by an oncoming Winnebago. It was no one's fault. The retired Canadian driving the camper said he didn't know what he'd hit until he saw Fleming's crushed Road King in his sideview. By then, there was nothing to be done."

Drew squeezed her hand. They'd been infidels for more than a year before Fleming's last ride, having taken advantage of his traveling ministry, and his trust, to indulge in their prideful charade. What fools they'd been to believe they could keep such a thing a secret from him. After so many good works, Fleming was surely seated at God's right hand, if God could be said to exist at all. If such were the case, could it be that he was tailing them now? Drew had pondered this as they'd sped from Tucumcari up Highway 54 across the panhandles of Texas and Oklahoma into Kansas, a phantom Fleming in his rear-views, silver crucifix detailed onto his black front fender, torso ensconced in black Tri-Armor, bearded chin and shaved scalp hidden within a black Schuberth C3 Pro, the soles of his boots like wings sprouted from his chrome triple clamps, only to vanish when Drew tried to look at him directly.

"Sounds like he died doing what he loved," Marc said.

Before Fleming had found God, Jen and he had regularly returned to the law firm Fleming had founded and at which they all worked with tales of the roadside attractions at which they'd stopped, from the World's Largest Celtic Cross Carved from a Single Rock to the Groundhog Zoo and Home of Punxsatawny Phil, from the Bronze

Statue of Chef Boyardee to Jolly Jim the Mystery Tree, and from Big George the Howitzer to the Monster of Unfathomable Pedigree. If Fleming liked a place, he called it trippy.

"You know, here's something that might help a little with the grieving," Marc said. "For several years after you and Corey visited us, we'd receive a postcard from him every now and again, and not the postcards we sold him, mind you. No, ma'am, I believe these were postcards purchased from other vendors that appealed to him for one reason or another, that he enjoyed. It's why, I guess, I never forgot him. Why, I recollect receiving one of Oak Cliff, Texas, where Lee Harvey Oswald offed J. D. Tippit, another of a Giant Mailbox in Newellton, Louisiana, yet another of the Future Birthplace of James T. Kirk, located in some small town in Iowa the name of which eludes me, I'm afraid."

The points of Marc's vest jiggled on either side of his Northrup King belt buckle. "James T. Kirk, captain of the Starship Enterprise. His future birthplace. Now doesn't that just beat all?"

"It's in Riverside, ten miles south of Iowa City," Jen said. "The future birthplace is behind a hair salon. Down the street from it is a bar and grill. In the back of the place, on the floor beneath the pool table, is a plaque engraved with the date of Captain Kirk's foretold conception, June 22, 2227—the joke being that his parents, as yet themselves unborn, will make love, at least once, on that very felt."

"Mind bending," said Marc and slapped a

bronze National cash register with ivory keys and raised fleur-de-lis adorning the sides and drawer, a relic upon which Fleming would certainly have commented, for no one had appreciated a curiosity more than he until he didn't anymore.

At the far end of the museum opened the maw through which the Dalton boys had evaded capture, a rough-hewn crossbeam supported by posts and a narrow passageway lit by intermittent bulbs. Why had he brought her there, Drew asked himself. Was he jealous of the happiness she and Fleming had known during their courtship and the early years of their marriage? Did he want proof that the life he and Jen were making together would never hold a flame to what she and Fleming had known? He'd thought it an act of mild rebellion, to see whether he might gain access to a past that wasn't his and shouldn't have concerned him. But the more Marc and Jen talked, the more he felt as if Fleming and he were locked in a stranglehold, the years that had passed since Fleming had brought her there collapsing into the space separating warriors conjoined in mortal combat. Drew could smell the day-old Folgers Fleming favored, the musk he slapped across his cheeks and chest, even the breath mints that lolled around in his mouth as Fleming examined legal briefs over Drew's shoulder.

"Cory took you there, too," Marc said.

"Where didn't we go?" Jen replied and mentioned a few of the places they'd biked together: the Hormel Plant in Austin, Minnesota where Spam was made, The Peggy Lee Museum in

Wimbledon, North Dakota, The World's Largest Rubber Band Ball in Eugene, Oregon, The Giant Frogs on Thread Spools in Willimatic, Connecticut. Those were just a few that came to mind, she said, neither the best nor the worst, and Marc's eyes seemed to spark with recognition. Had Fleming sent him postcards of those places, too?

Before Fleming's death, when he and Jen had kept their liaisons secret, the hidden places the world offered seemed interconnected and limitless, darkened alleyways that led to gritty motel rooms that looked onto side streets and vacant lots none in their right minds ventured. Their homes were forbidden, since anyone might see them coming or going, and while they'd first made love on the pleather sofa in his office, work was too risky, with court reporters, plaintiffs, and defendants camped in the lobby during business hours and cleaning crews and infrared security cameras compromising their privacy once doors were barred for the night. After that, they'd stuck to the shadows, to pay-by-the- hour motor lodges that catered to customers who didn't care about cable, or if the carpets needed replacing, or the drapes were stained, or he parked his Tahoe behind dumpsters big enough to eclipse it. In industrial blight from which most averted their eyes, he and Jen treated their love as if it were a rare flower, a cave-dwelling blossom that would wither and die if exposed to sunlight, and he already missed those days.

"This might interest you. Three years ago, a smart young lady about your age came in just as you have done and slapped one of our post-cards on the countertop. I thought she'd taken it from the dispenser and intended for me to ring it up, which I did, and said, 'Miss, that'll be a dollar five.' That's when she flipped it over. I recognized Corey's chicken-scratch right away. 'I'll be,' I said. Come to find out her name's Lanny Turnbull, daughter of Frank and Delores Turnbull of the Turnbull Ranch up near Buelah, Wyoming, and a trustee of the Turnbull Buffalo Jump Foundation. During the construction of I-90 back in the 70's, a sinkhole used as a killing pit by the Apache, Shoshone, Crow, and Cheyenne was discovered on their property."

"We went there, too," Jen said and described an archeological site off the freeway. Dating as far back as the 1500's, Native American hunters had stampeded buffalo off the edge of it. The "jump" was over 200 feet wide and 100 feet deep, and in it, preserved in layers of red earth, were the bones of over 20,000 bison as well as remnants of the arrows and knives used to slaughter and butcher them. "Funny. I remember Lanny, too. She was manning the desk that day. Fleming and she started talking about astrophysics, core-collapse supernovae, and the like. Before that, they'd been discussing religious fanaticism and doomsday cults and the theory that what the Book of Revelations really describes is a galactic astronomical event not likely to happen for another fifty million years."

Was there any obscure point of interest to which Drew could take her that Fleming hadn't already? As far as he knew, they hadn't left the continental U.S. of A. Yet as he imagined the attractions to be found across the plains of Saskatchewan, the lake country of Ontario, the vast tundra of the Northwest and Yukon Territories, or as they zigzagged southward through the Sierra Madre Occidental, Oriental, and del Sur, the Mexican Altiplano and Trans-Mexican Volcanic Belt to the jungles and beaches of the Yucatán, it was as if Fleming were delighting in forcing them further and further afield. Arcane Americana had been Fleming's passion, and he'd canvassed it so thoroughly that anywhere Drew took Jen was sure to contain trace elements of their prior visit.

"Corey made quite an impression on Lanny, too. Bought one of every postcard she had in stock, just as he'd done here, only when she started receiving postcards from him a few weeks later, postcards of various attractions he'd wandered into and liked for one reason or another, she started driving to a few of them herself, to see what separated them from the dross, what made them special or unique. It was why she'd come here. Would you like me to tell you what she discovered?"

"I don't know," said Jen.

"Well," Marc said, "not everyone she met remembered Corey, but some did, and a few like me had even saved the postcards they'd received from him, postcards that made them wonder whether their attraction might be a part of a network visible to a discerning few, that despite their own doubts about the place, they were maybe, just maybe, doing something right. You ask me, your old man was on to something, connecting the like-minded, letting them know that their commodity was appreciated, and that others were just as committed as they were to providing the public a quality roadside experience."

"I had no idea," Jen said. "I doubt my late husband did either."

"It gets better. Some of us, the Turnbull Family, the Meade County Historical Society, the Rattlesnake Roundup folks over in Rangum, Oklahoma, the Beer Can House folks down in Houston, the Birthplace of Philo Farnsworth, the Father of Television folks out in Beaver, Utah, to name but a few, formed an, albeit loose, alliance based on Corey's recommendations. We have an Internet presence. You can visit us at www.coreystoppedhere. com. To become a member, you must either be addressed in a postcard you received from Corey or your establishment must be depicted on one he sent to a bona fide member. It's as simple as that. If you or a member can provide photographic evidence of the postcard Corey sent—it must bear a postmark as well as Corey's distinctive if illegible signature—you're in. That's all there is to it."

He'd asked her once what she thought had happened to Fleming, why he'd lost interest in the law firm, in him, in her, in them, and she told him that she didn't know but didn't hold it against him either. "If he were anybody else," she said, "I'd be irate, but Fleming's different. He doesn't operate on the same plane as you and me. He was, I think, put on Earth for a higher purpose."

"The problem was," Marc said, "because Corey never included a return address on any postcard as far as we know, none of us knew how to contact him. If we had, we would've thanked him from the bottom of our hearts and offered him free admission to all roadside attractions in the collective for the rest of his natural life."

Earlier in the day, talking to each other on the radio, Jen had said, "It's like he's lieutenant again, our protective caboose."

"His ghost?" Drew asked.

"I think he's forgiven us and wants us to take joy in each other now that he's no longer with us."

That would've been uncharacteristic of the Fleming Drew knew. The firm that Fleming had founded litigated legal malfeasance suits, and he would return not as their guardian angel but as a dark lord demanding retribution. True, Fleming had been born again, true as well that charisma once employed to great effect in the courtroom transferred well to the gospel tent, true that his flock consisted mainly of bikers and that over time he came to prefer them to his clients, most of whom just needed convincing, at a rate of $200 an hour, to drop their unwinnable cases. But from the winnable ones, the ones on which Fleming had staked his reputation in a legal community that made pariahs of attorneys who prosecuted their own, he knew that Fleming would stop at nothing, perhaps not even eternal damnation, to right so egregious a wrong.

And yet one evening after the three had

gone together on a long ride and while ambling up the steps into a saloon in Tombstone, Arizona, he'd said to Drew, "I love you, man. I'll always love you, and there's nothing you can do to ever change that," and kissed him, and Drew remembered how against his shaved cheeks the man's fulsome lips and bristly mutton chops formed a live wire through which divinity had charged into him, thrilling him nuts to nipples. There was no other way to describe it.

Marc grinned. "While I can't speak for the collective as a whole, it would please me to offer free admission to the Dalton Gang's Hideout to you and your. . . ?"

"Consort," Drew replied.

Twice divorced with a grown daughter who loathed him, he was so ordinary, so typical, despite his efforts not to be. He didn't even know who the Dalton boys were much less what crimes they'd committed. He would've told Jen she was right—he had no business crashing a past that didn't belong to him—and suggested they leave right then had it not begun to storm in undulating sheets that lashed the knoll that sloped to the street.

Jen thanked Marc for his hospitality and led Drew to the entrance of the tunnel. "When U.S. marshals arrived," she explained, "the outlaws fled from the farmhouse to the barn and escaped on horseback, the lawmen none the wiser."

"What were they wanted for?" Drew asked.

"Train robberies mostly," Jen replied. "Only Emmett survived the great attempted bank raid despite taking twenty-three rounds to the arms, legs, and chest. He served fourteen years in the pen and went on to become a famous Hollywood author and actor."

In the tunnel, the smell of ozone mixed with that of lacquered pine. Thunder cracked, electricity singed the air, and the string of bulbs lighting their way blinked off. Marc called to them down the shaft, "Don't panic, friends."

They were in total darkness, and in such quiet Drew could hear his own heartbeat. "It's Fleming," he whispered. "He's all around us. Don't you feel him?"

Though she would later claim neither to have said nor to have heard anything in the silence that followed—she was, she said, reciting the rosary in her mind and clutching her silver cross and necklace of beads—he would swear on his deathbed the word, "Trippy," fell from the dead man's lips.

"I love you, man. I love you," Drew said, and when the lights came back on, he was on his knees, alone, blind, and blubbering like a child.

After Logic

In 5th grade I was taught to play chess by Mr. Dornseif, the father of five boys, three of whom—John, Jim, and Tom—I considered my friends. John was my age, but Jim, two years older than me, was my best friend while Tom, a year older than Jim and a bona fide teenager, was ensconced in a cloak of mystery, the 45 rpm of Black Sabbath's "Iron Man" spinning endlessly on a turntable behind the locked door to his basement bedroom and grumbling up through the struts and beams of a 1950's Rambler into the paneled office where Mr. Dornseif and I sat face-to-face in Naugahyde chairs on either end of his ash and walnut chessboard.

A tall, lumbering man inclined to tan business suits that never quite fit him properly or, on weekend afternoons after tinkering on the mahogany 1923 Ford Model T he was building with his sons in the garage and with time for a quick game, a pair of ratty, grease-stained khakis and a nylon, geometric-patterned sports shirt, Mr. Dornseif didn't feel at home in his body. I could tell by the way he picked at the sores on his freckled forearms, ran his fingers through the thin, red strands that slalomed across his pale dome, and breathed through his mouth in moist gusts that condensed into a kind of dew on the chessboard. Perhaps I did not feel at home in mine either, at ten chubby, uncoordinated, and acne-prone, and could see something of my own discomfiture in him. I know I felt sorry for him without exactly knowing why. None of his older sons—to Billy and Stevie, then seven and four, a pawn was no different than a rook when thrown in a tantrum—liked him well enough to feign even a passing interest in the game while for me, whether I was white or black, on offence or defense, the off-putting aspects of Mr. Dornseif's personality—and they were legion—melted away, and it was as if he and I were in the presence of each other's soul.

Perhaps I'm overstating it, how the awkwardness between us vanished as each calculated the possible variations resulting from a knight-to-queen-seven or a bishop-to-bishop-five, all the while envisioning an end game in which one of us would declare, as if only winning granted one license to speak, check and checkmate! But I don't think so.

For more than a year I was Mr. Dornseif's faithful disciple, learning to play chess by learning how he played it, and lost one close game after another. For Christmas that year my parents bought me a chess set, one I'd chosen myself from the Sears catalogue, with plastic pieces in a dull, matte finish and an oversized, laminate board that I set up on a TV tray beside my bed, so that each night before falling asleep I could solve (or try to) the daily chess problem I cut from the Minneapolis Tribune. With allowance money I purchased Bobby Fisher Teaches Chess, a bestseller, but I'd advanced beyond its elementary lessons and gave it to my homeroom teacher, Ms. Woodruff, who in her wavy skirts and tops was keen to take part in the craze. Not surprisingly, I thought about chess at the exclusion of friends and family, angering Jim who accused me of "using" him to get to his father and eliciting the concern of my own father who told me one night before bed, as I was reenacting the Polish grandmaster Akiba Rubenstein's stunning obliteration of fellow Pole Gersz Rotlewi in Lodz in 1907, that he and my mother had discussed the amount of time I was spending at the Dornseifs and agreed there was something "peculiar" about Mr. Dornseif's interest in playing so much chess with me.

"You don't understand," I told him.

"What don't I understand?" he replied. He'd turned around my swivel desk chair and was sitting on the other side of my chessboard, his slacks crossed at the knees, in the same proximity to me as the unsuspecting Rotlewi had been to Rubenstein as the latter sacrificed his queen in a breathtaking gambit that led to mate three moves later. But to my father, an M.D. released from the Army after two years of conscripted service, chess had no relation to real life, and I didn't know what to tell him. Racquetball with friends and bridge with my mother against other couples were as close as he ever came to needing an opponent to complete himself.

To complete himself? As soon as I thought this I broke out in a sweat, knowing I could never say it aloud to anyone: yes, when we played chess Mr. Dornseif completed me. What I said to my

father I don't recall. Probably I told him our
games were exciting, that Mr. Dornseif and I
were a good match for each other, that although
I'd come close to beating him on two occasions, I
hadn't beaten him yet. I imagine my father was
satisfied with my answer, for he didn't pester me
about it again that night. So, on Saturdays after
breakfast I dashed from our house, cut through
our neighbors' backyards to the loop on which
the Dornseifs lived, and rang the doorbell in time
to eat a second breakfast of blueberry pancakes,
scrambled eggs and bacon, strawberries and
muskmelon Mrs. Dornseif had prepared in quan-
tities to satisfy a lumberjacks' camp.

When I sat down at the empty chair and
made us a table of eight, Mr. Dornseif intoned,
"Come, Jesus, be our guest and let these gifts to us
be blessed," and no one said their "Amen" with
more conviction than I. Then platters were passed
from hand to hand until every plate was filled. It
wasn't that my own mother didn't prepare break-
fasts just as hearty and delicious; it was that in the
Dornseifs' household I could become someone
other than I was in mine, someone who surprised
himself with how courteous and helpful he could
be, someone who cleared not only his own plate
but the plates of others and, once all were in the
sink, rinsed them and put them in the dishwasher.

During a phone conversation Mrs. Dornseif,
my mother's first friend in a new community that
prized, above all else, appearances, commented
upon this to my mother, who upon reporting back
to me said, "I wanted to tell Marcia she must've

confused you with someone else." I was bounding up the stairs to my bedroom with Mr. Dornseif's copy of Richard Réti's Masters of the Chessboard, which he'd loaned to me that afternoon after claiming yet another narrow victory, and I was ready to devour the chapter on Adolf Anderssen and the Falkbeer Gambit, which Anderssen employed with great success against the mathematician Jakob Rosanes in Breslau, Germany in1862. "She also said that Roy thinks you're a genius."

I halted between floors. "Mr. Dornseif thinks I'm a genius?"

"I'm just reporting the news," my mother replied. In the kitchen I found her sprinkling caraway seeds on wieners she'd wrapped in crescent dough and arranged on a baking sheet. This was how I knew that she and my father were dining out that night and that I would be left for the evening to look after my sister and brother, which, for a dollar an hour, was worth it to me back then.

"What did she say exactly?" I asked.

"Now I wish I hadn't said anything," my mother replied, but through the curtain of auburn hair I could see the dimple cupping the corner of her upturned mouth.

That night, after pigs-in-a-blanket, macaroni and cheese, and chocolate pudding and once Elaine and Gus were in front of the television beguiled by Bewitched, I did the unthinkable. I phoned the Dornseifs, and when Mr. Dornseif answered, I asked him if he wanted to play a second game of chess that day.

"Tonight?" he said.

In the background Elizabeth Montgomery in the role of Samantha Stephens told her mother Endora, played by Agnes Moorehead, that she and her husband Darrin, played by Dick Sargent, were in the midst of a discussion about their daughter Tabitha's education when with a grand sweep of her chiffon sleeve Endora produced from a puff of smoke Professor Poindexter Phipps—just as she did in the living room in which my sister and brother lay on our olive shag like frogs.

"Why sure," he said. "Come on over, why don't you? The boys will be happy to see you. And afterward I'll make us root beer floats. How's that sound?"

"Great," I said, "if I weren't stuck at the house babysitting my sister and brother—"

"Wait," said Mr. Dornseif, his voice a whisper. "You want me to come there?"

"No, sir," I said. "I mean, yes, sir."

"Hold on a second, will you, Travis?" As I'd turned the dial on our wall-mounted phone, I'd had no inkling of the uneasiness I would feel actually inviting Mr. Dornseif to our house to take part in time-honored recreation. As it was, it was an uneasiness I wouldn't experience again until junior high and high school when I'd muster the courage to phone and ask on dates girls who'd given me no indication they were interested in me at all.

"Travis," he said in a whisper, "I just spoke to Marcia. She thinks I'm going to an ad hoc meeting of the Model T Club of America. I'm secretary of our local chapter."

"Ok?" I said.

"Which means I'm all in," he whispered. "Go ahead and set up the board. I'll be there in ten."

"It's set up now," I said. On the kitchen table the rows of white and black pieces were faced off as if for a Medieval conflagration.

"Now no small talk before the game. Tonight, it'll be just chess. And Travis?"

"Yes?" I said.

"Let's keep this between ourselves."

Over the phone and from the living room, as if the scene were broadcast in stereo, Darrin told Samantha, "Because around here after logic usually comes disaster," followed by a laugh track.

"Sure," I replied. If Mr. Dornseif's desire for secrecy was lost on me, I also didn't want to scare him off.

We hung up, and I told Elaine that Mr. Dornseif was coming over to play chess. She was in 2nd grade and, back then, obeyed my every command. "For some reason," I said to her, "he doesn't want his wife to know."

"Mrs. Dornseif?" said Elaine.

"Yes," I said, "and I want us to respect his wishes. Do you understand me?" She nodded, and I said, "That means no telling Mom and Dad that Mr. Dornseif was ever here."

She nodded again, and I showed her my approval with a quick smile she craves to this day. "I feel sorry for him," I said.

"I do, too," she said.

"His sons hate him," I said.

"I know."

•

These many years later I still remember the wet April snow falling as I let Mr. Dornseif in through our front door, the Buick Estate Wagon I never noticed when it was parked in his driveway looking alien and strange parked in ours, the chrome Sweepspear above the woodgrain glinting in the porch light as the smell of oil smoldering in its V-8 engine wafted into the house with him. In the entryway he stomped the snow from his galoshes and, balancing on one leg and then the other, flipped each with a grunt beside the row of winter boots beneath our Amish mission bench, and though it made no sense to me, I had the distinct impression of having admitted a menace into our home.

"Chess on a Saturday night?" he said. "Inspired, Travis. Just inspired."

By then Elaine had tucked Gus into his crib upstairs in our parents' bedroom and, to give us privacy, was watching "The Mary Tyler Moore Show" on the small Zenith black and white they kept on the credenza at the foot of their bed. Today she has no recollection of Mr. Dornseif ever being inside our house without our parents there and certainly not of me, on the verge of definition, asking Mr. Dornseif for his lambswool overcoat and muffler and, once he'd handed them to me, hanging them in the hallway closet between the snowmobile suit our father wore ice-fishing and the mink stole our mother had donned the one time they attended the opera.

In the kitchen I asked Mr. Dornseif whether he'd like something to drink. He said, "Milk," and I asked him, "two percent or whole?" He said, "Whole," and I poured us each a glass. As I set one before him, he held out pawns in his cupped fists. I tapped the left and drew black. "Ready to have your heinie whipped?" he asked, which he asked every time we played, and usually I replied, "Ready to have yours?" But aware of how voices carried, I said nothing, and he opened with pawn-to-queen-four, and I responded with knight-to-king's-bishop-six, the standard Indian Defense to his Queen's Pawn opening. We traded pawns, and in our battle for control of the middle squares, I lost a knight but took a bishop, drawing his queen from hiding. From then on, it was as if a new pathway had been forged in my brain, I could see moves beyond what he could, and nothing he did surprised me. I forked his rook and queen, took his rook, and mounted a protracted assault that was at once vertical and diagonal and from which his king had no escape, but as my vision stretched to an outcome that lay beyond the reach of his, it was as if I could look back at him over my shoulder and see him huffing and flailing, with no idea how he'd wound up married to a woman he didn't love and who didn't love him, in an executive office at I.B.M. for eight hours a workday spearheading projects he had to pretend he understood and supervising personnel who couldn't dumb down their work enough for him to understand it, and during his free time, under the chassis of his beloved Model T on a mechanic's creeper, asking for a clutch gap tool and being handed an external band adjuster, asking for a plate rivet and being handed a clutch pedal support bolt, only the oldest, Tom, knowing the difference between the mail ordered parts but, high on the weed he dealt at school, thinking it funny to pass the wrong one to the youngest, Stevie, who, having carried it on his hands and knees into the glow emanating from the work lamp dangling from a rod ball socket, had to bear the full force of their father's wrath—"I'm raising imbeciles!"—though, to be fair, Stevie always reemerged grinning, clear to him whose team he was on.

If I pitied Mr. Dornseif, I couldn't take pity on him. I couldn't throw the game. With my remaining rook, I put him in check. He could've protected himself with his knight, but chose to tip over his king instead, the inevitable as clear to him as it had been to me moves ago.

"You did it, Travis," he said. "You bested me." Slumped in a chair with his knees spread, he looked spent, his eyes watery and pink. "You know," he said, "I think highly of you, Travis."

"I think highly of you, too, Mr. Dornseif," I said.

"But it's more than that for me," he said. "You're what I want in a son. My sons—" He trailed off. "Well, you know them." He sniffled and wiped his eyes. "Look at me. I'm a mess. This is no way for a man to act. Your father, if he saw me, would run me off the property, as well he should."

"No, he wouldn't," I said, though, in truth, my father found him insufferable and at backyard barbecues and Easter suppers only tolerated him because Mrs. Dornseif and my mother had become such close friends.

He slurped the last of his milk and forced a smile. "I should go," he said and lumbered back to the entryway where I fetched his jacket and scarf from the closet.

He put his galoshes back on, and I held the door open for him. "Thanks for the game, Mr. Dornseif," I said.

"Thank you, Travis," he said and trudged through the falling snow back to his station wagon.

•

I never lost to him again, though for a time it looked as if our chess-playing days were over. Three days after I'd beaten him, my mother called me into the kitchen when I came home from school and told me I was henceforth grounded for the next two weeks.

"I can't believe you invited Roy into our home while your father and I were out," she said. "Roy? Of all people."

"Elaine told you?" I imagined the tortures I would inflict on her.

"Elaine didn't tell me. Marcia did."

"Mrs. Dornseif wasn't even supposed to

know," I said. "Mr. Dornseif told me he wanted us to keep it between ourselves."

"I'm sure he did."

"What's that supposed to mean?" I asked.

"Know what he did as soon as he got home on Saturday night?" my mother asked.

Our house sat on a hill, and through the window over the sink I could see through the gauzy elms, over the snowcapped rooftops of the Wilkens' and Heutmakers' houses, smoke from the Dornseifs' chimney curling into a question mark and dissolving into a slate gray sky. "He confessed to Marcia."

I felt angry and betrayed. "Confessed to what? Chess? A game I won, by the way."

"It's more complicated than that," my mother said. "The upshot is Marcia and Roy are separating."

"Separating?"

"It's what people do before they divorce, Travis."

"I know what it is."

"Let's go into the living room," my mother said. There she sat me at one end of a couch she'd reupholstered in wool broadcloth, the earth tone fibers of which matched our paneled walls and framed embroidery but against one's back felt like the wriggling antennae of an insect infestation. She sat down at the other end and said, "I'm going to be frank with you, Travis. Roy has a problem with boys, with liking them in a way that isn't good." Her chin quivered, and I could tell she was weighing what she had to tell me

200

against my capacity to understand it. "Something happened before they were married or maybe even started dating. I don't know exactly. Marcia wasn't very specific and, honestly, I didn't want to hear the details. But he confessed it all to her, and she made 'No time alone with a boy' a condition of their marriage."

Her eyes pleaded with me for affirmation that I'd grasped what she'd told me.

Though I didn't, not then anyway, I said, "Funny that she and Mr. Dornseif should have five sons and not one daughter."

This made her laugh. "I agree it's weird." She took a deep breath, then told me that under no circumstances was I to repeat what she'd told me to anyone. "Not a word to Tom, Jim, John, Billy, or Stevie, do you understand me? None of them has any idea their father's this way, though, imagine, for as long as Marcia and Roy have been married, he's had to see someone at Mount Olivet for counseling, a Pastor Swenson or someone."

I nodded, fearing if I asked her what "way" Mr. Dornseif was, she'd see how little I'd fathomed. So instead I thought about all the hours I'd spent at the Dornseifs' house and never once seen Mr. Dornseif alone with any of his sons, how even when the time came to affix the new Model T parts that had arrived that week, whether it was the drive shaft assembly consisting of a universal joint and dozens of special tools, nuts, gaskets, pins, and plugs or just the horn, he'd call all five by name from the top of the stairs and the job would be done as a group activity, whether it took three minutes or the better part of an afternoon, with Mr. Dornseif detailing step by step what he was doing as if to students in a shop class. This was what had made being in the garage with them all so painful. Mr. Dornseif spoke to none of his sons as individuals, but as if he couldn't tell them apart.

"But maybe Mr. Dornseif is getting better," I said. "When we play chess at his house, we're always alone together."

"You might think you're alone," my mother said. "But let me assure you, Marcia's right next door in the kitchen or there in Roy's office with you."

As I thought back on all the chess Mr. Dornseif and I had played, what my mother said was true. There hadn't been a game during which Mrs. Dornseif hadn't brought us something on which to nibble, lemon snowdrops or Berlinerkränser or petticoat tails, then collected the tray sometimes before we'd even tasted a cookie. Or she puttered around Mr. Dornseif's office, dusting his bookshelves and desk, spending extra time on the teak desk plate he'd brought home from work. It was engraved with the word "THINK," and she'd hold it up to the window as if checking the brass for smudges. In light of what my mother had told me, had Mrs. Dornseif been trying to communicate with her husband?

To issue him a warning?

What I didn't know then was that Mr. and Mrs. Dornseif would stay together and that when he completed his Model T it would be the pride

of the neighborhood's Fourth of July parade, fes-
tooned with banners and flags and filled with
children catapulting red, white, and blue popcorn
balls onto the lawns. I accepted my grounding be-
grudgingly, and as one day joined the next, I grew
to appreciate my confinement, solving chess prob-
lems, replaying historic chess matches, and otherwise working on self-improvement. I unearthed
my barbells from my closet and, between bouts
on the chessboard in which I tried to play white
and black simultaneously and with equal fervor,
I performed dead lifts, shoulder presses, curls,
and squats. As I reflected upon what my mother
had told me, it occurred to me that, despite all I
hadn't understood, Mr. Dornseif liked me—he'd
told me so himself—and, unless I'd been utterly
hoodwinked, he found me physically attractive.
Maybe even sexually so. I was by then a pudgy
eleven-year-old with an oily complexion. No one
found me sexually attractive. That Mr. Dornseif
did made me think others might, too, and I imagined myself metamorphosing over the course of
a decade-long exile into a cross between Sergio
Oliva and Alexander Karpov. With the brawn of
the former and the brains of the latter, I might, I
thought, one day find love.

Anything You Recognize

Detective Noriega drove us through the jungle in his Jeep. Mandy rode shotgun, and I sat in the back seat with the ice chest. It was 1982, and Mandy and I had traveled together from Kodiak Island, Alaska to Mexico's Yucatán Peninsula, by thumb, bus, rail, and taxi, only to have our backpacks stolen as we'd snorkeled and sunbathed. The robbery had occurred late on the very day we'd arrived at what we hoped would be our final destination, Tulum, and upon returning to the cabana we'd rented for the week and in which we thought we might stay the winter, we found ourselves the butt of a cruel joke. Everything but what we'd taken with us to the beach was gone, and ingress hacked through a bamboo wall with what we imagined machetes opened into a drapery of vines. It was as if our packs and the fallout that had erupted from them while digging for our fins and masks had been tapped by a magic wand.

Noriega's arm lay across the backrest of the passenger seat as he steered us over winding tire ruts through a menagerie of green-tinged shadows, his camouflaged sleeves rolled to just below his elbows, his epaulettes starched and taut. I kept an eye on the fingers of his right hand, across which Mandy's soft, brown curls fluttered in the down draft from the windshield, waiting for them to fondle her neck or ear. Sticking out from between the driver's door and seat, the staghorn handle of his Colt .45, which he'd bragged was the same model as the single action revolver given to George Patton when he came to Mexico with General Pershing to capture Pancho Villa sixty-six years before, was so close I could've caressed its engraved grip. Would I dare to yank it from Noriega's holster, say, "Stop right there, buster," or sit quietly by, pretending he wasn't actively seducing my traveling partner, someone I wanted to think of as my girlfriend now that we'd finally, just the night before and for the first time ever, made love?

With no rearview mirror, there was no way to see how uncomfortable he was or wasn't making her. They chatted cordially, as if oblivious of me behind them. He wanted to know where she'd grown up and, upon being told, "Garden City," claimed never to have heard of it.

"It's on Long Island," she said.

"Ah, Long Island," he said as if thinking fondly of the iced tea. When we'd reported the burglary earlier that morning, Noriega was the only one manning the Municipio Registro Civil, and I was taken aback by how attentive he was to us, wanting to know where the robbery had occurred—El Paradiso Resort, Cabana 5—what our backpacks looked like and an accounting of everything in them and around them at the time of the break-in. How many pairs of long pants, how many pairs of shorts, long-sleeved shirts, hats, t-shirts, dresses, skirts, bras, pairs of underwear, socks, shoes, sandals, boots? We listed everything we could think of, including the long underwear, the woolen caps and sweaters, we'd needed in Alaska. What about I.D.'s, he asked and frowned when we told him the thieves had made off with our passports and driver's licenses, too. Not good, he said. Not good at all. Money?

Mandy and I glanced at each other. We'd secreted our earnings from a summer and fall spent processing salmon and king crab in secret pockets we'd sewn with monofilament between the packs themselves and their detachable aluminum frames, three grand a piece in crisp Benjamins the teller at the Kodiak Branch of the First National Bank of Alaska had counted out for us once we'd stepped off the seaplane with our settlement checks in hand.

We nodded, and Noriega looked up from his desk, his sharply manicured mustache standing out on a face scarred, I imagined, years ago by an exploding pane of glass. "How much?" he asked, and we told him, ashamed of our stupidity. Why hadn't we brought the money with us to the beach? If we'd thought to bring even half of it, sealed in watertight pouches belted to our waists or worn around our necks on lanyards, our situation wouldn't be half as dire.

"That's a lot of lettuce," Noriega agreed and signed his name at the bottom of the form on which he'd recorded our description of the incident. "Now let's see if we can find your backpacks."

"Now now?" Mandy asked.

"No time like the present," he replied, and as he stood up from his wooden desk, he retrieved his cannon of a revolver, holster and all, from a bottom drawer. He held it reverently before him, as if a priest were standing by with holy water, and buckled it around his waist. "It's like American Express," he said. "I never leave home without it."

Now Mandy was saying, "But it's been years—oh my word, eight—since I've been to the east coast," and listed the places she'd lived since leaving New York and meeting me on the salmon butcher line of Columbia-Wards Fisheries' remote Alitak Plant—Manitou Springs, Colorado, Cannon Beach, Oregon, Maui—leaving out the abortion or two she'd had at each, the last one paid for by Robert, a home builder and commercial pot grower with whom, she claimed, she was still in love, though he was married and had a son and daughter under the age of ten. She was twenty-six to my twenty-one, and if in the past weeks we'd traveled more than 5,000 miles together, I'd butted my brain against her ageist contention that she couldn't be romantic with anyone not older than her by a decade or more until my head and heart both ached.

If the interlude of the night before had been a wondrous anomaly, spurred on by the trauma we'd experienced that afternoon, I knew better than to interpret it as a sign that anything had changed. Since awaking in our cabana at dawn and swimming in the sea to jar ourselves from groggy complacency, Mandy had made no mention of our lovemaking, and neither had I, afraid she would tell me that it hadn't happened, that I had made it up just as I had all the other memories of sex with her, and I would have no choice but to agree.

At the start of our journey, I'd told her that if our partnership was to remain platonic, she couldn't stop me from imagining the sex we might've had along the way. That it was actual sex we'd had made it, strangely, no different from the sex I'd imagined us having now that it was a memory.

"Beer?" Noriega asked her. Mandy told him no, thank you, and Noriega asked me to grab one for him from the cooler. I fished a can of Tecate from the ice and handed it to him. "It's Miller Time somewhere, no?"

He yanked the tab and arced it over his head into rainforest I worried would provide our final resting places. Granted, paperwork left at the station tied us to him, but if he wished to have his way with Mandy and make me watch, he could kill us both afterward, destroy any evidence of his ever having met us, and be home in time for a supper of sopa de lima. As he drove, I kept imagining pulling back the elephant ear ferns, the lowest of many canopies that umbrella-ed the earth, and finding bodies beneath them. We'd been warned of the trouble we could get into with the police. They were in cahoots with the drug cartels all over Mexico, but in Tulum, given its proximity to Guatemala, the problem was especially bad. Every traveler we'd met had a tale of woe, but if this was ours, would we even live to tell it?

In a stand of guanacaste trees around the trunks of which bone-white liana vines had en-wrapped themselves in towering sepulchers that stretched to a frondescent ceiling through which sunlight filtered in spindles, Noriega squashed his empty Tecate can into a disk on the dashboard and flung it into foliage that engulfed it like a frog a fly. He stopped the Jeep, and in the space be-tween his seat and door, his knuckles flashed, and he was pointing his long-barreled revolver at the sky.

"To let the bandits know we are here," he said.

He pulled the trigger, and the report re-sounded as if the coastline itself were fissuring from the continent.

"Jesus," Mandy said.

He seemed almost giddy as he climbed from the Jeep. "What're you slowpokes waiting for? Maybe in the U.S. stolen property grows legs and returns to its owners like a lost dog. But down here, we go get it."

Mandy turned to me with fear in her eyes. "We have no choice," I murmured and climbed from the vehicle, too.

We could've turned and run, Mandy in her purple flip-flops, me in my leather huaraches, both of us in our still-damp swimsuits, but if Noriega meant to kill us it made little difference whether we were moving targets or stationary ones. Still, maybe this was how robbery investiga-tions were conducted down here, I thought, hold-ing out hope as Noriega waved us on, threading a path through brush that switched back into our faces, under and over fallen timber splotched with fungi the pink of pitahaya, the yellow of star fruit, the scaly green of sweetsop, the gargantuan root systems unearthed on either side of us looking like lairs of petrified snakes.

A Yucatán jay, wings and tail the blue of sea foam, flitted from branch to branch ahead of us, and in time I confused it with the actual sea as it appeared first as emeralds and sapphires scattered before treasure hunters lured to the cave of their demise, then, as the jungle receded behind us and we entered a coconut grove, a tropical lagoon.

Before us lay a makeshift campground in the sand and sea grass, tents set up in an oval around a grated fire pit from which wisps of smoke carried the aromas of breakfast. Woven hammocks, like the ones sold in Merida and stolen from us, were contented grins slung between the palms, and a hundred yards beyond them more than a dozen people frolicked in pools as pellucid as the iris of an eye. Noriega fired his gun again, and the blast echoed up and down the shoreline as if the scene were recurring in other secluded coves, to others like us.

All heads turned to us. The shouts, laughter, and sounds of mirth extinguished, men, women, and children emerged nude from the sea, the lot fair- skinned, sinewy, and tall. Water dripped from their breasts and genitals. "Warum? Warum?" asked one of the men in whose wizened beard, pubic bush, and silver hair pink flowers were entwined. "Warum belästigen sie uns?"

His eyes pleaded for an answer, but Noriega gave him none. Instead, he fired his gun a third time, and the Germans retired to their tents as if familiar with the routine. They hauled out what possessions they harbored there—flashlights, cooking utensils, toiletries, foodstuffs, camping supplies, books, clothing, backpacks of various shapes and sizes—and set everything before us in a pile on the ground.

"Zufrieden?" the man asked.

A boy of six or seven walked up to Mandy and extended his hands to her, in them a limpet shell smaller than a pea. "Why, aren't you a dear," she said. A jeweler inspecting a semiprecious stone, she held it to the sunlight, then turned to me and mouthed, "Did you see that?" her eyelids fluttering like moths in water, and I thought of the five abortions she'd told me about, each pregnancy a flame of hope for as long as it took her to realize she'd either have to douse it or raise the child herself. The way I saw it, a lover shouldn't have to be a father first.

Noriega scooped a halter-top from the mound and asked her if it was hers. "It's pretty," she said, "but it isn't mine."

"How about this?" Noriega asked her, in his hands a cocktail dress, low-cut, slit to the hip. He turned it around, displaying a crimped, crepe bow. "It would look lovely on you, darling. You know, for dancing in Cancun? Tripping the night fantastic?"

"We're not going dancing," she said.

"No?" Noriega said and rifled through more

clothing until he found a lavender bustier corset with steel buckles down the front and laces down the back. "Perhaps this is more your style? For the after-hours clubs?" He tossed it to her, and she caught it with one hand. "If it fits, it's yours."

"It isn't mine," she said, "and I'm not trying it on."

Noriega smiled. "If you'd like, I'll look away, but as you can see, normal rules don't apply here."

"Didn't you hear me?" she replied.

"Suit yourself," Noriega said and turned to me. "Anything you recognize? Anything here belong to you?"

It all could've; I had only to say yes.

•

Afterward we stopped for tacos at a roadside stand. Noriega handed us a beer a piece from the ice chest, and we waited for him at a picnic table on the side of the shack while he ordered at the service window. Mandy wanted to know why I was pinching myself, and I said, "For proof we aren't dead."

"Maybe we are," she said, "and just don't know it yet."

"Those poor German nudists. I don't believe they ever stole anything from anyone—"

"Amigos!" Noriega exclaimed as he sat down next to me and across from Mandy. As if dealing cards, he distributed our tacos to us in red plastic baskets, each with sides of salsa and guacamole, beans and rice. Behind us sat a table of telephone line repairmen in hardhats and reflective aprons, their utility vehicle with hydraulic lift parked beside them. "After lunch, we'll pay visits to two other crime rings—one French, the other Dutch."

Mandy looked Noriega in the face. "The Germans didn't steal our stuff," she said. "And I doubt the French or the Dutch did either. No, I think you know exactly who ripped us off, but you're either too tight with them or scared of them to do right by us."

"Watch your mouth," Noriega said. "You don't know who's listening." He bit into a taco and wiped his lips with his napkin, smiling all the while. "I can tell you know nothing about how things work down here."

"I know enough," Mandy replied.

"Then I'm afraid I've done all I can for you." He finished his meal. "You'll need an Informe de Incidentes." He removed one from his breast pocket and, after filling it out, went back over it dotting each 'i', including the one in his name. "If anyone asks for your identification, you show them this. It explains why you have none. If they have questions, tell them to dial this number and ask to speak to Sergento Primero Fernando Noriega."

He underlined the number and slid the form across the table to Mandy, who thanked him as much for his candor as his thoughtfulness, but, in only her swimsuit and the blouse she'd worn to the beach when our backpacks were stolen, had nowhere to put it. From the tote containing, among other things useless to us now, our snorkels, masks, and fins, she extracted my copy of Sartre's Being and Nothingness and inserted it between leaves earmarked and coffee stained.

"May I take you back to town?" he asked, and we told him no, that we would begin hitchhiking back to the States from where we were. We were on Federal Highway 307, on the outskirts of Filipe Carillo Puerto, when Noriega bid us goodbye. "Adios!" he yelled, waving at us from his Jeep.

"Do you think," I whispered once he was gone, for I'd grown suspicious of the linemen at the picnic table behind ours, "that he's going to tell the robbers exactly where to find our money?"

"Maybe," Mandy said and began to hyperventilate. I told her not to, told her that we were travelers and this was our tale, promising her that one day we'd find it so funny we'd tell it to our kids, which made her laugh, though exactly why I couldn't say.

Acknowledgements

A book is a community effort, and I'm grateful for the help this one received from all sorts of people: Jon Roemer at Outpost19; Richard Peacock and Nita Congress at Gargoyle; Chris Lukather at The Writing Disorder; Robert Stapleton and Susan Lite Lerner at Booth Journal; Amy Yelin and Richard Hoffman at Solstice: A Magazine of Diverse Voices; Kristian Macaron and Justin Bendell at Manzano Mountain Review; Barrett Warner at Free State Review; Elizabeth McKenzie at Chicago Quarterly Review; Ron Spatz at Alaska Quarterly Review; Kate Gehan at Pithead Chapel; Robert Vaughn and David O'Connor at b(OINK)/Bending Genres; Katherine Jackson for the opportunity to share my work at the ODU Lit Fest, a highlight for me of the early days of the pandemic; University of New Mexico's English Department and Creative Writing Program; the Low-Residency MFA Program at Queens University of Charlotte; Tinker Mountain Writers' Workshop; UNM Hospital's Cardiac Unit; Fred Leebron; Jim McKean; Chris Powell; Brittany Wade; Barbara Jones; Thorpe Moeckel; Jeff Kleinman; Pinckney and Laura Benedict; Hal and Melissa Ackerman; Melissa Basher; Gisele Firmino; Anita Obermeier; Sharon Oard Warner; Greg Martin; Julie Shigekuni; Andy Bourelle; Steve Benz; Jonathon Davis-Secord; Marisa P. Clark; Lisa D. Chavez; Marissa Greenberg; Gary Harrison; Matt Hofer; Scarlett Higgins; Sarah Townsend; Jesse

Costantino; Finnie Coleman; Scott Sanders; David Dunaway; Gail Houston; Jack Trujillo; Eva Lipton-Ormand; Levi Romero; Dee Dee Lopez; Dylan Gauntt; Val Lacey; Susan McAllister; Vanessa Haye; Larry Goeckle; Jan Bowman; Toby Tucker Hecht; Rayne Ayers Debski; Maggie Duncan; Jane Gatewood; Betsy Ashton; Robin Haase; Janet D'Eredita; Ron Yates; Mike Burrell; Michael Noltemeyer; Faerl Marie Torres; Amanda Kooser; Mia Coleman; Keith Hood; Richard Vargas; Dan Darling; Nari Kirk; Dawn Sperber; Carmella Starace; Melanie Unruh; Michelle Gurule; Finnegan Shepard; Jane Kalu; Amarlie Foster; Jenn Tubbs; Tyler Mortensen-Hayes; Suzanne Richardson; Tatiana Duvanova; Brenna Gomez; Andrea Gollin; Bernardine Connelly; Ted Corcoran; Nancy Kober; Avery Chenoweth; David McNair; Suzy Chamandy; Karen McElmurray; Linda Dunn; Peter Ho Davies; Cindra Halm; Lailee Mendelson; Will Sexton; Paul Harding; Darrach Dolan; Mathew Liebowitz; Jeanne Larsen; Nancy Naomi Carlson; Faith Shearin; Tom Murdock; Adrienne Su; Dan Manheim; Lisa Briana Williams; Wendell Ward; Amy Seader; Kelly Fordon; Yemani Asmerom; Jerome Hartwig; Harry Stecopolous; Eleni Stecopolous; Tom and Julie Coash; Robert Harllee; Thadd McQuade; Brad McCarthy; Jean Collins; Steve and Emily Quane; Lester Sanders; Jessa Herren Walker; Mindy Nathan-Blaize; Jen Monroe; Kristi Aiken Christman; Sharon Ramirez; Melissa Barnes; Doug Garder; John Behling; Ellen Shepard; Mark Hopkins; Dorsey Griffith; Ranja Sem; Joey Retzler; Susan Hankla; Paul Lisicky;

Elizabeth McCracken; Heidi Jon Schmidt; Roger Skillings; Cynthia Huntington; Cleopatra Mathis; Polly Burnell; Jenny Humphreys; John and Barbara Hersey; Yael Dougherty; Burt and Marguerite O'Neil; Regina Wong; Sylvia Tsao; Ketu and Mitu Patel; Nancy, Sue, Paula and the rest of the Left Mirror Gang; Gianna Mendoza and Rick Aldighieri; the Back Corner Crew (Susan, Chris, and Steve); the KDJ Social Club; Rebecca Louise Goddammit; Alison Wheeler Knipe; Susie Baker; Tosca Lee; Mick Smuk; Tim Godfrey; Jeff Rick; Andrew Gifford; David Morrell; Sheila Lamb; Susan Baker Buie; Adam Abrams; Anthony Swofford; Shawn Behlen; Angela Bills; Nick Gronewald; my sister-in-law Beth Brooks; my brother-in-law Ken Mandel; my brother Kurt Mueller; my sister-in-law Shalini Shankar; my nephew Roshan Shankar-Mueller; my niece Anisha Shankar-Mueller; my sister Karen Mueller-Sparacino; her partner-in-crime Tony Harvath; my mom Linda Mueller; my stepfather John Sciamanda; my dad Jim Mueller; my lovely and amazing daughter Lili Rosano-Mueller; and the answer to all my dreams Michelle Brooks. This book is for all of you.

About the author

Daniel Mueller is the grateful recipient of fellow-ships from the National Endowment for the Arts, Massachusetts Cultural Council, Fine Arts Work Center in Provincetown, University of Virginia, Iowa Writers' Workshop, and Sewanee Writers' Conference. He teaches on the creative writing faculties of the University of New Mexico, Low-Residency MFA Program at Queens University of Charlotte, and Tinker Mountain Writers' Work-shop.

Printed in the USA
CPSIA information can be obtained
at www.ICGtesting.com
BVHW041918040823
668224BV00003B/18

2 370011 551661